Elaine had been crying, he
startled to realize.

"Tell me what's wrong." He knew she would probably consider this an extreme infringement on her personal life, but at this point he didn't care.

She looked at him through bleary, swollen, red-rimmed eyes. "I'm fine," she whispered, not convincing either of them.

It never failed. When someone was in trouble, Brent felt the uncontrollable urge to go to the rescue. No matter how irritating the damsel in distress.

"No," he said gently. "You're not." She looked like hell, which was amazing to him considering she usually looked as if she'd just stepped off the cover of a fashion magazine.

"Okay, Brent, you really want to know?" A small, self-deprecating laugh hiccuped past Elaine's lips before she choked on another sob. "I'm pregnant."

Dear Reader;

Silhouette Romance begins the New Year with six heartwarming stories of the enduring power of love. Felicity Burrow thought she would never trust her heart again—until she met Lucas Carver and his darling little boy in *A Father's Vow*, this month's FABULOUS FATHER by favorite author Elizabeth August.

Love comes when least expected in Carolyn Zane's *The Baby Factor*, another irresistible BUNDLES OF JOY. Elaine Lewis was happy to marry Brent Clark—temporarily, of course. It was the one way to keep her unborn baby. What she didn't bet on was falling in love!

Karen Rose Smith's emotional style endures in *Shane's Bride*. Nothing surprised Shane Walker more than when Hope Franklin walked back into his life with a little boy she claimed was his. Loving little Christopher was easy, but trusting Hope again would prove a lot harder. Could Hope manage to regain Shane's trust and, more important, his love?

The sparks fly fast and furiously in Charlotte Moore's *The Maverick Takes a Wife*. When Logan Spurwood fought to clear his name, Marilee Haggerty couldn't resist helping him in his search for the truth. Soon she yearned to help him find strength in her love, as well....

And two couples discover whirlwind romance in Natalie Patrick's *The Marriage Chase* and *His Secret Son* by debut author Betty Jane Sanders.

Happy Reading!

Anne Canadeo

Please address questions and book requests to:
Silhouette Reader Service
U.S.: 3010 Walden Ave., P.O. Box 1325, Buffalo, NY 14269
Canadian: P.O. Box 609, Fort Erie, Ont. L2A 5X3

THE BABY FACTOR

Carolyn Zane

Silhouette
ROMANCE™
Published by Silhouette Books
America's Publisher of Contemporary Romance

Dedication: To the Lord, with many unending thanks for blessing
us with Madeline Alexa, our own little Bundle of Joy.
Thanks to: My mother, Mary Patricia, for everything.... And to
the doctors, nurses and birth class at Newberg Hospital, who—
thankfully—in no way resemble the characters in this book.
Acknowledgment: Last but not least, Doug and Bob, for the
brainstorming sessions.

 SILHOUETTE BOOKS

ISBN 0-373-19127-8

THE BABY FACTOR

Books by Carolyn Zane

Silhouette Romance

The Wife Next Door #1011
Wife in Name Only #1035
**Unwilling Wife* #1063
**Weekend Wife* #1082
Bachelor Blues #1093
The Baby Factor #1127

*Sister Switch

CAROLYN ZANE

lives with her husband, Matt, in the rolling countryside near Portland, Oregon's Willamette River. Their menagerie, which included two cats, Jazz and Blues, and a golden retriever, Bob Barker, was recently joined by baby daughter Madeline. Although Carolyn spent months poring over the baby-name books, looking for just the right name for their firstborn, her husband was adamant about calling her Madeline. "After all, Matt plus Carolyn equals Madeline." How could she resist such logic?

So, when Carolyn is not busy changing Maddie, or helping her husband renovate their rambling one-hundred-dred-plus-year-old farmhouse, she makes time to write.

Bundles of Joy

Dear Reader,

When I married my college sweetheart, we were barely more than bundles of joy ourselves. Wisely, we agreed to put off having a family until we were out of college. We knew how much time children could take. After college, we decided to wait until we had established our careers. We knew how expensive children could be. After the careers took off, we decided to buy and remodel our first home. We knew how much room children needed. After we remodeled the first house, we were exhausted. Let's travel, we said, before the children come. We knew how hard it would be to travel with children.

Throughout the years, friends and family would urge us to get started on that baby. We would look at each other and smile knowingly. We knew misery loved company.

Finally, we ran out of excuses, and last summer, on our sixteenth wedding anniversary, we welcomed Madeline Alexa to our family. And with her awesome, miraculous birth, we learned something that only this gift from God could teach us. No college degree or career, no house or vacation, nothing material this world has to offer could ever equal the magic this tiny bundle of joy has brought to our lives.

I wish you the happiness and love with your families that we have found with ours.

My best,

Prologue

"You're pregnant."

Dr. Hanson nodded over his bifocals as he tossed Elaine Lewis's file onto his ink blotter. "Congratulations." He smiled reassuringly at her and, groaning, settled his aging frame into the seat behind his desk.

Elaine blinked and attempted to focus her eyes away from the many framed diplomas and certificates on the wall. She was certain her heart had stopped beating as she digested her obstetrician's staggering announcement.

"Oh." Somehow she'd managed to overlook the obvious symptoms.

However, considering the severe emotional trauma she'd been through this past month, it was no small wonder. Her hands moved stiffly to the expensive silk scarf she wore knotted at her throat.

What in heaven's name am I going to do now? she wondered, numb with shock. She tugged at the colorful knot in an effort to fight back the wave of hysteria that threatened to finally send her over the edge.

This was too much. Her eyes darted wildly around the room as her brain tried to compute and file this latest bit of devastating data.

She was pregnant. With child. She, Elaine Lewis. Single, powerful, network television executive. Pregnant at thirty-three.

This wasn't how it was supposed to happen. This is not what she had planned at all. Although, nothing in her usually well-disciplined life had gone according to plan since the first of the year.

Her voice shook as she leveled her gaze at the older man. "You're sure?"

Dr. Hanson chuckled and folded his hands comfortably over his generous abdomen. "I'm sure. In fact, I want to see you back here in four weeks for your first prenatal visit, okay? Until then," he scribbled quickly on his prescription pad, tore off a sheet and handed it to her, "I want you to take one of these vitamins every day, watch what you eat, no alcohol or tobacco, and keep the heart rate below 120 beats a minute when you exercise. Any questions?"

No. Yes. Was it too late to back out? she wondered frantically, running the palm of her hand over the suit jacket that lay so snugly over her flat stomach. *What have I done?*

"I guess not," she answered dully, as the stark reality of what she now faced began to dawn on her.

"Okay. I'll see you next month then." Dr. Hanson rose from his seat with a broad smile and extended his hand. "Congratulations, Elaine. You've all worked so hard for this moment. I know how happy you must be."

Happy? Unfortunately, Dr. Hanson didn't know the tragic truth yet. She fought the irrational urge to laugh. No, happy didn't begin to describe the barrage of emotions that she felt. She was going to have a baby. Unfortunately she had no desire to be a mother.

Too shell-shocked to even try to explain the mess she now found herself in, she nodded weakly, shook the doctor's hand and headed in a depressed fog toward the door.

Once outside in the parking lot of Chicago Central Hospital, she leaned unsteadily against her Jaguar and inhaled great gulps of fresh, morning air. A stiff spring breeze whipped across the lake, tugging tendrils of hair loose from her smooth chignon and blowing them into her eyes. She fumbled for a moment with her keys and finally succeeded in opening her door.

Rigidly she held her tears in check. She couldn't lose it now. Over the past month she'd managed to hang on to her precious control through the most horrifying weeks of her life.

Her orderly, regimented routine was the only thing that had kept her from a complete and total nervous breakdown. And it would keep her from falling apart now, she thought, angrily swiping at an errant tear that had managed to squeeze past her tightly shut eyes.

Sliding into the leather-upholstered interior of her car, she shoved her key into the ignition and took yet another deep, steadying breath. She would just have to deal with all of this later, she decided, stoutly refusing to give in to the desperation that clawed at her throat. Thinking and feeling were luxuries she couldn't afford. Right now she had to get back to the station and begin producing Chicago's premiere five-o'clock news show.

The show that would still go on, even though she, the producer, was pregnant.

Chapter One

"Elaine?"

Taking a deep breath, Elaine stopped in her tracks and then exhaled in irritation. The last thing she wanted to do was stand in the hallway and make idle chitchat with one of her reporters. Why they called it morning sickness was beyond her, she thought, feeling her cheeks and forehead with the back of her hand. It was late Friday afternoon, and she still felt positively green.

"Yes?" She hoped her tone conveyed her reluctance to dally.

Brent Clark's dark head popped out of the editing bay into the hallway, and he squinted at her through his horn-rimmed reading glasses. "When you have a minute, I need to talk to you." He grinned cordially.

It looked like he had cut his hair with a weed whacker or some other equally blunt-bladed farm equipment. She was going to have to have a talk with him. Maybe out there in corn county—or wherever it was that Clark hailed from—a reporter could get away with that windblown haystack look, but not here.

"Can it wait for a few minutes?" She doubted it would take very long to throw up the crackers she'd managed to eat for lunch. She felt as if they were trying to swim upstream now.

Brent shrugged with the easy-going, laid-back charm that—for reasons that continued to boggle her mind—delighted the Chicago population at large. "Sure." He nodded affably and leaned back to allow his production assistant into the room with a cup of coffee.

The smell of the java was her undoing. "Good," she managed to say, before turning and tearing down the hallway toward the ladies' room.

Brent shook his head slightly and pushed his hair away from his face. If Elaine didn't slow down one of these days, she was going to end up suffering from some kind of stress-related health problem.

"Here, you look like you could use this."

"Thanks, Debbie." Brent took the steaming cup of coffee from the perky, young production assistant's hand and shifted his attention back to the video monitor.

Debbie peered over Brent's shoulder in the cramped editing bay of the newsroom at WCH. "What are you working on?"

"I'm putting the finishing touches on a fire safety series that will air late next month during May sweeps."

"Wow. Some fire," she breathed and scooted in closer for a better look. "This should win the spring ratings battle."

He could feel Debbie's warm breath tickle the hair at the back of his neck. The young girl made no secret of her crush on him, but, as cute as she was, he wasn't interested. She was just a little too fresh off the cheer squad for his blood. "Mmm." Taking a swig of his coffee, Brent shook his head and ran a weary hand over his jaw. "We shot this five or six weeks ago, when that high-rise condo on the shore of Lake Michigan burned down."

Debbie's wide blue eyes narrowed thoughtfully. "Oh, yeah. Now I remember."

"Tragic. Never should have happened. These exclusive high rises," he said, pointing to the flaming apartment complex on the screen, "aren't supposed to burn like that. The local building codes require sprinklers these days. This must have been an older building. Slipped through the cracks, I guess." He shrugged.

At times like these, Brent almost wished he'd gone into another profession. Sometimes it seemed like there just wasn't any good news left to report, and the rash of fires he'd covered lately didn't do much to improve his outlook. Today he felt far older than his thirty-four years.

Sighing sadly, Debbie shook her head. "Didn't a bunch of people die in that fire?"

"Yeah. About a dozen. There were at least six people living on the top floor that didn't make it out." Brent searched forward on the tape. "You can see why."

The sound of his lanky cameraman flopping down into the seat next to him drew Brent's eyes.

"Man, I'm bushed." Ray Freed yawned noisily at the ceiling. "I'm gettin' too old for these all-nighters. How does the stuff we shot in the wee hours look?"

"Terrific." Brent referred to the footage of yet another fire that they had shot late last night. "You do good work, my man."

"Too bad The Barracuda will find some reason to rag on it." Ray snorted and mimicked Elaine. "Why didn't you get closer? Why didn't you get some interior shots? Videotape doesn't melt *that* easy."

"Geez, Ray, why don't you talk a little louder? I don't think they can hear you down in the studio." Brent cast Ray a sardonic look and the cameraman grinned sheepishly.

It was true, Brent thought, Elaine was a demanding producer. But she wasn't as bad as Ray made her out to be. She was the reason their show was number one, and everyone knew it. She certainly didn't deserve the title they hung on her behind her back, he mused. Okay, so she was tough as nails, but he suspected that—somewhere beneath her rather unapproachable demeanor—she had a softer side she didn't bring to the station. And, Brent grinned to himself, for a barracuda she had great legs.

Ray glanced around nervously. "Where is Elaine, anyway? I haven't seen her all day."

"She said something about having another one of her mysterious doctor's appointments this morning." Debbie grinned. "Maybe she's having the barnacles scraped off her rusty little heart."

"Or maybe we'll be really lucky and she has a terminal case of lockjaw." Ray twisted in his seat and winked back at Debbie.

Brent's mustache quirked in aggravation. "For your information, she's back. In fact, she should be here in a few minutes. Why don't you guys go find something constructive to do, instead of sitting around griping about the boss?" he muttered, scowling at them.

Throwing her hands up in exasperation, Debbie said, "I don't get you. Why do you always defend her? You know she thinks you're nothing but a country bumpkin. You're her star reporter and she treats you like something she stepped in out in the barnyard."

Brent grinned at Debbie's righteous indignation. It was true. Elaine, when she bothered to notice him at all, tended to peer down her delicate nose at his Iowa broadcast experience. He knew, being the new kid on the block, that he had to pay his dues.

Though sometimes it really rankled him that she saw him in a less savvy and sophisticated light than his hip, happening, designer-clad co-workers. Nobody else held his small-town background over his head the way she did.

However, it was not in his nature to bad-mouth the boss behind her back, no matter how superior her attitude.

"Come on, Deb." Brent remonstrated. "If you can't say something nice..." Although, he had to admit, when it came to Elaine, he could understand how the young woman would be hard-pressed to come up with something. Especially lately.

"Ha," she retorted huffily. "I think you have a thing for Ms. Barracuda. Too bad." She ruffled his overlong hair and looked at him appreciatively. "I bet when you take off these ridiculous glasses, style this mop of yours, trim your mustache and put on an outfit from this decade you're adorable." She turned and grinned at Ray. "The gals in the secretarial pool say his rugged good looks make all the other reporters look like sissies."

"Macho man!" Ray thumped Brent good-naturedly on his large bicep.

Brent squirmed under their scrutiny.

"Yeah. A real heartthrob." She wriggled her eyebrows suggestively. "Anyway," she said, incredulous, "I just don't understand why you always stick up for the one woman who thinks you're a complete corn dog. What is it with you men?" Her sigh was heartfelt. "You need to get your priorities straight, doll face."

"Thanks for the free analysis, but if you don't mind, I have work to do." Just because he didn't want to hop on the gossip bandwagon and play shred the producer, didn't mean he was in love with the woman, for crying out loud. Brent pulled his reading glasses off and tossed them on the table. Stretching, he rolled his head tiredly from side to side and trained a bleary eye on Ray and Debbie. "So," he waved his hands at them, "get outta here, will you?"

Ray clumsily levered himself out of his chair and grabbed Debbie's hand. "I can tell when we're not wanted. See you at The Pub for a couple cold ones tonight, Brent?" The cameraman referred to the small Chicago microbrewery around the corner where the WCH news gang—with the exception of Elaine—gathered every Friday night after work.

"Yeah, sure," Brent mumbled distractedly. "Whatever." Shrugging them off, he went back to his project. It was nearly perfect. Hopefully Elaine would agree.

As he transcribed some of the comments the fire marshall had to say, he wondered why Elaine had gone to the doctor. "Barnacles scraped off her heart." He chuckled to himself and shook his head. Well, even though Elaine could be a complete and total pain in the neck at times, he hoped with all his heart that she was okay.

"You didn't wear *that* in the piece you shot last night, I hope," Elaine snapped, taking in Brent's rumpled appearance. Squeezing into the editing bay, she stood beside him and stared in frank disapproval at his clothing. It had been a long day for her. Nausea, meetings, nausea, doctor's appointment, nausea . . . she was in no mood to deal with the slovenly work habits of her staff.

Brent shuffled through his notes and nodded absently. "It was dark when I got dressed in the middle of the night, and I was in a hurry. Besides, my clothes are barely noticeable."

Elaine, annoyed at his lack of concern, said, "You could take a minute to turn on the light. You're representing WCH for crying out loud. We have an image to maintain."

Brent's chair squeaked as he dropped his head back and sighed up at her in exasperation. "Elaine, the place was burning down. I didn't have time to worry about making a fashion statement."

Glancing at the image on the screen, she blanched and felt the blood drain from her cheeks. Good Lord. Not another fire. She gripped the edge of the counter and, swallowing the urge to scream, waited for the sudden wave of nausea to pass. It was okay. She was a big girl. She could handle this.

"Well—" she blinked away the last of the black dots that danced before her eyes "—at least get a haircut." Her eyes drifted to the thick, dark locks that fell in an unruly mess across his forehead. "And when you get home, toss the corduroys, okay? It looks like you wore them in high school."

"I did."

Shaking her head she ran a fluttery hand over her abdomen.

She had yet to adjust to this pregnancy thing. And what on earth would her staff think when she announced that she was with child? Farm boy here, would probably drop dead from corn-fed horror.

Maybe she would keep it a secret and let everyone think she was getting fat. What the heck? Just another reason for them to make snide remarks about her behind her back.

"I was just putting the finishing touches on part one of the fire safety series." He punched the Rewind button. "And I wanted to get your feedback. Want to take a peek?"

No! she wanted to shriek. But she couldn't. Instead she glanced at the clock and wished she had an excuse to avoid sitting through a program that—for personal reasons—would be hell for her to watch.

"I guess so." Pulling a chair up beside him she sank tiredly into its seat. "Okay," she said, feeling like a wilted flower, "let's get this show on the road."

Brent shot her a curious look as she fidgeted.

Casting him her haughtiest I'm-your-superior-so-mind-your-own-darn-business expression, she stared pointedly at the screen. "I haven't got all day."

Searching back to the beginning of his piece, Brent leaned forward and nodded at the footage that flickered across the screen. "We got a few really fantastic shots out of some stuff we had on file. And the shots Ray got last night will fill in nicely. Some of these sound bites are real tearjerkers."

Elaine nodded uneasily, and her heart began to pump faster than the images that sped backward across the glowing monitor. She was incredibly uncomfortable with the subject matter of his series.

Even so, she had to give Brent his due. He may have earned his stripes reporting out in the boondocks, but his stuff was always on the cutting edge. Feeling sicker with each passing moment, she tried to feign a serene interest in fire safety.

"I bought a brand new shirt and tie, just for this series." He smiled genially at her as he cued his tape to the opening segment. "No corduroys on camera."

She bobbed her head curtly as the story began. "Good."

Brent's thoughtful, engaging copy drew her into the story as it unfolded, and again she was forced to admit that he was good at his job. They were extremely lucky he'd joined the news team at WCH last year. And, even though his small-town charm and easy-going manner made him a hit with the Chicago audience, she couldn't seem to resist giving him a hard time about being from Iowa. Sometimes he was just such a hick. Glancing over at his frown of concentration, she wanted to smile. Until the images on the screen pulled her back to reality.

As the camera zoomed out to reveal the facade of a flaming building, Elaine stiffened and felt her pulse begin to roar in her ears.

No. It couldn't be.

"Uh, Clark." Calling him by his last name, her voice cracked as she stared in morbid fascination at the screen. "Back up. I want to take another look at that last shot." The sudden wave of sickness that had washed over her had nothing to do with her condition.

Brent backed the tape up and sent Elaine a questioning look.

She felt faint. "When did you shoot this?"

"Waverly Towers? About a month and a half ago. You were out of the office for a couple of days, so I never got a chance to show it to you...."

"I don't want you to use this," she said suddenly. Trembling so violently she could hardly speak she whispered, "Take it out, okay?"

Brent's brow furrowed in confusion. "Oh, uh...why?"

Her head spinning dizzily, she had to force the words past the fingers of doom that squeezed her throat. "Because I don't like it."

Brent drew his lower lip into his mouth in consternation. "Hey now, wait just a minute here, Elaine. This scene is integral to the—"

"I don't care. Just do it," she barked. Abruptly standing on shaky legs, she walked from the room, leaving him to stare after her with raised eyebrows.

* * *

"Another round for my friends." Stuart Aldridge, another of WCH's evening news reporters, tossed his credit card grandly onto the table and lifted his glass to the group in celebration. "Here's to a stellar series on fire safety. May it save many lives, and kill the competition during spring sweeps."

Stu saluted Brent and the rest of the WCH crew who had gathered at The Pub after that evening's show. The crowded establishment was filled to bursting with the Friday night, after-work set.

"I'll drink to that," Ray shouted above the din and clinked his glass noisily into Debbie's. "That series ought to make The Barracuda sit up and take notice. What happened to her, anyway?" he asked curiously, and handed his empty glass to the harried cocktail waitress. "I saw her tear out of the editing bay this afternoon like she was running from a fire. Looked a little freaked," he mused, tossing a peanut into the air and attempting—unsuccessfully—to catch it with his mouth.

Brent rubbed his darkened jaw and frowned. "I don't know. She told me to eighty-six a shot in part one of the fire safety series, and then she never came back." Another opportunity to impress her down the tubes, he lamented, and reached for a handful of peanuts.

"That figures." Debbie looked disgustedly around the table. "We bust our butts working late into the night to put together a darn good story to win her all kinds of acclaim for May sweeps, and we don't get any credit."

"What's this 'we' stuff?" Ray said crabbily. "I didn't see you there last night serving up a pot of that sludge you call coffee."

Debbie pursed her rosy lips in annoyance. "Hey, I make great coffee. Besides, you know what I mean. Brent knocks himself out putting in overtime, and she doesn't notice. Typical." She leaned chummily against Brent's shoulder. "But I noticed, honey. You were great, as usual."

"Thanks." Brent smiled at Debbie. "I just hope she's okay." He'd never seen his unflappable boss so shaken up.

"She has been going to a lot of 'doctor appointments' lately," Debbie confided smugly, tossing her juicy tidbit out to her inquiring-minded audience.

"I'd lay odds on an ulcer. You just can't live at the station the way she does. Any takers?" Ray tossed some bills into their traditional Friday-night betting pool.

Brent shook his head. "I think there's a lot more to it than that. She never gets that upset over a simple piece of video."

Stu snorted. "What rock have you been living under?" Opening his wallet, he dug out a bill. "I've got five that says it's a hangnail. That would explain the thorn in her paw lately."

"Oh, sure. That would explain everything." Brent's mouth curved in wry humor as he set his glass down and pushed back his chair. The noise, smoke and insipid gossip were beginning to get to him. It was time to call it a day. "I'm beat. See you clowns Monday morning."

"You're not going dancing with us?" Debbie whined, her lower lip protruding petulantly.

"No." Brent stood. "But thanks for the invite. I have some stuff to wrap up back at the station before I turn in for the night. You guys have fun, though."

"You're going back to the *office?* Aww, buddy. Get a clue," Stu advised. "Come with us and let us perk up that corpse you call a social life. We'll show you how it's done in the big city." He high-fived Ray across the table. They bayed and barked at the ceiling, causing the eyes of amused patrons to turn to their table.

"No, thanks." Brent smiled affably and slung his jacket over his shoulder. Big-city night life held no appeal. It was at times like these that he wished he had a loving wife and a passle of kids to head home to, instead of after hours at the station and then his lonely, cheerless apartment. "Some other time." Waving at his rowdy co-workers, he threaded his way through the hazy room and set off for the station.

Brent paused outside Elaine's office and noticed a dim light glowing from under her door. Glancing at his watch, he was surprised at the late hour. What was she still doing here? She worked far too hard. Ray was probably right. If she kept up this pace, an ulcer would be the least of her worries.

He hesitated, wondering if he should poke his head in and say hello. If he mentioned the time, she may take the hint and head home for the weekend. Wherever home was. He didn't know much about Elaine's personal life. No one at the station did. She was an extremely private person.

It was rumored, however, that she didn't have much family. He had that in common with her. And from what he could tell by the schedule she kept at the station, she didn't have much of a social life, either.

Oh, hell, he decided, as he buttoned his down ski jacket. She probably wouldn't appreciate any interference from a lowly employee. Especially from this lowly employee. He could tell Elaine wasn't the type who took kindly to well-meaning advice. "Her loss," he said under his breath.

Reaching into his pocket, he pulled out his wool scarf. The spring evenings still had a bit of a bite, and it had smelled like rain outside.

Better let stubborn bosses lie, he decided, and turned in the dim hallway to leave. The eleven-o'clock news crew was still here. Someone from security would undoubtedly make sure she made it to her fancy sports car in one piece.

As he moved away from her door, he thought he heard the sound of a muffled cry. Cocking his head, he tried to figure out where it had come from. Another sorrow-filled sob reached his ears, and he backed up several paces. Who would be here crying at this time of night? he wondered and waited for the sound to continue.

Again, the haunting, anguished cries reached his ears, leading him directly back to Elaine's door. Someone was crying in Elaine's office. Someone obviously in a great deal of pain. Was it Elaine?

He vacillated.

Should he knock? Or should he just go in? It was a tough call. Knowing Elaine—if it was Elaine—she would probably want to be left alone. Too bad he couldn't summon the wherewithal to force his feet to move. It was a character flaw he couldn't seem to overcome. When someone was in trouble, Brent felt the uncontrollable urge to go to the rescue. No matter how irritating the damsel in distress.

Standing helplessly outside her door, he listened to the pitiful, heart-wrenching sobs. Aww, geez. He hated it when women cried. Oh well, might as well get this over with, because there was no way he could leave now and still have his conscience intact.

At his tentative knock, the crying stopped.

"Yes?" came the feeble query.

It was Elaine.

"Uh, Elaine? It's me, Brent." He could feel his heart pick up speed.

"Oh." She sniffed. "What can I do for you?" she called, her voice breathy with emotion.

He pushed the door open. "I was…uh…just passing by and thought I'd say good-night. Are you all right?"

She eyed him through bleary, swollen, red-rimmed eyes. "I'm fine," she whispered, not convincing either of them.

"No," he said gently. "You're not." She looked like hell, which was amazing to him considering she usually looked like she'd just stepped off the cover of *Cosmo*.

Closing the door quietly behind him, he crossed the room and sat down in one of the plush leather chairs situated directly in front of her large, executive desk. Her office was opulently decorated, the walls adorned with numerous awards and photos of her with various celebrities and local officials. Unfortunately the tragic figure seated behind the desk looked anything but a powerful executive.

"Tell me about it," he coaxed and at the same time wondered what the heck he was setting himself up for.

She didn't seem to notice his breach in office protocol. "No, I'll be all right."

The reporter in him surged to the surface. Brent studied her tear-stained cheeks and knew she was lying to save face for some reason. She was far from all right. In fact, she'd seemed far from all right for weeks now. Call him a masochist, but he made up his mind he wasn't leaving until he found out what the problem was.

Taking a deep calming breath, he decided to take a chance on Debbie's comment about her many trips to the doctor of late. He knew she would probably consider this an extreme infringement on her personal life, but at this point he didn't care.

"Did you get some bad news from the doctor?" His fingers tightened imperceptibly on the arms of his chair, and he hoped that this wasn't the case. Good grief, what would he say if she announced that she was dying?

She shook her head and mopped the tears that welled in her eyes with the sleeve of her silk blouse. "No, really, thanks for your concern, but I'm—" she tried to smile "—healthy."

That was a relief. But whatever it was that bothered her was obviously serious business, and he could see that she needed to talk about it with someone. She seemed so alone.

"Elaine." He spoke the single word with a heart full of compassion. He knew what it was like to be alone, even in the middle of a crowd. "What then?"

Leaning forward in his chair, he braced his elbows on his knees and let his hands dangle between his legs.

As though figuring she had nothing to lose by confessing to him, she slumped pathetically across her desk top and plucked at her damp sleeves. Her breathing was jerky, wracking her slender body as she fought for control.

She stared blankly at Brent and began to speak.

"You know that...um, fire you covered about a month and a half ago?" she asked, her voice barely audible in the intimate hush of her office after hours. "The one I told you to cut today?"

"Yes." He answered softly, not wanting to interrupt.

She opened her mouth to speak, but swallowed a sob instead.

Brent waited as patiently as he could for her to continue, an unknown fear gripping his belly.

Drawing on her waning inner strength, she continued. "I, uh . . . knew two of the people who died. In fact," she whispered, "I was related to them."

He closed his eyes, feeling her pain. He could understand now, why she'd been so upset recently.

A small, self-deprecating laugh hiccuped past her lips before she choked on another sob. "And to make matters worse—" she trained her large, tearful, brown eyes on him "—I'm pregnant with their child."

Chapter Two

Elaine twisted the soggy tissue in her hands and surreptitiously studied Brent for his reaction. Thankfully, he didn't look appalled or disgusted at her predicament. That was something she didn't think she could take.

Instead he sat in silence and allowed her to cry. Handing her tissues from the box on her desk from time to time, he waited quietly for her to continue. It was evident that he wanted to help somehow, and curiously, she was grateful.

Up till now, Elaine had never felt the need to confide in anyone. She'd always considered that a sign of weakness. However, as of a month and a half ago, she was left completely alone in this world. No family. No friends to speak of. And, because there was no one else to share her grief with—and because he was there—Brent was elected.

"She was my cousin." Elaine sighed raggedly. Her eyes darted to her hands and then back up to Brent's gentle face. "Sara, and her husband Bobby Johnson, were the only family I had left. My parents passed away several years back."

Nodding sympathetically, Brent drew his ankle up over his knee and settled in to listen.

"I guess there was so much...smoke." Her throat constricted, and she shut her eyes, temporarily unable to continue.

"I know," Brent murmured. He'd been there. He remembered.

"And," she breathed, when she was able to speak, "I never even got to say goodbye. I never even got a chance to tell them—" her voice dropped to a whisper "—about their baby. Oh, dear God." Elaine buried her face in her arms and let the despair overtake her for a moment.

Brent felt his own heart grow heavy with her sorrow.

She looked up to find him watching her, compassion filling his face. Never in a million years would she be able to explain why she suddenly wanted to spill her guts to him. Must be part of the reason he was such a good reporter.

She brushed her hair back from her face and blew her nose, attempting to pull herself together. "They were so young," she continued, and felt her eyes glaze over as the memories flooded back.

"Sara wanted a baby more than anything. Bobby, too." Elaine's smile was tremulous. "Personally, I can't imagine that." She shook her head.

"But Sara was different. The only problem was, she couldn't get pregnant. They tried everything science had to offer. Then Sara got the idea to ask me to act as a surrogate. Bobby agreed since he had no family to speak of, either, with the exception of his mother, and from what I gather she wasn't exactly surrogate material."

Leaning forward Brent nodded and, intent on her words, encouraged her to continue.

"At first I wanted nothing to do with their crazy plan." Her chin tilted stubbornly. "After all, I'm busy with my career. Far too busy to become involved in their problems.

"So they continued to explore other avenues—adoption, other surrogate options—but nothing seemed destined to work out. All the while, Sara kept badgering me. 'C'mon,

Lainey' she'd say. 'Please just consider it. Who better to carry our baby than someone we love?'"

The tiny lines at the corners of Brent's eyes crinkled softly. He leaned his elbow on the armrest of the chair, cupping his jaw in his hand, fully engrossed in her compelling story.

Tears trembled on her eyelids, blinding her as she shook her head. "Anyway—" she sighed and allowed her head to drop against the back of her chair "—when my thirty-third birthday rolled around, I realized I wasn't getting any younger. I knew I probably wasn't the type to ever marry and have children of my own, and something inside of me just seemed to snap. The old biological clock, I guess," she reflected, lost in the past. "Curiosity must have gotten the better of me, because I decided that with this plan, I could have the experience of pregnancy and childbirth, and none of the responsibility."

"Why?" Brent asked, unable to stave off the reporter's need to know. "Why didn't you want to get married and have a family someday?" Shoot, if he could find the right person, he'd love nothing more than to do just that. He'd never be able to understand why anyone in their right mind would actually choose career over family.

She smiled a tiny smile. "That's a loaded question with about a dozen different answers. Suffice it to say that my own mother gave up a brilliant career as a concert pianist to marry my father and raise me. And she never let either one of us forget it." Her laughter echoed hollowly around the room. "She made sure that I learned from her mistakes and did something with my talents. Besides," her smile was defensive, "like my mother, I don't exactly think the wife and mother routine is my forte. And I love my job. I'm good at it."

Brent nodded in agreement. It was true. She was good at her job.

"Anyway," she said haltingly, and steered herself back to the original subject, "it seemed perfect. Her egg, his sperm, my body. I would be able to satisfy my biological urges, go back to my orderly, executive life, and Sara and Bobby would become parents. So we saw a lawyer and drew up an agreement. I wanted to make sure that my responsibilities ended with the birth.''

Elaine took the tissue that Brent offered and wiped her eyes. She felt disoriented, lost in the surroundings of her own familiar office. Distant sounds of the city, an occasional siren and car horn, filtered up from the busy city below, where life went on, oblivious to the devastating situation within which she now found herself.

How could it be, she wondered, that the earth continued to rotate and people carried on normally, when her whole world had shattered? It all seemed so surreal. Slowly she lifted her heavy lids and stared at the man who sat patiently waiting for her to finish her story. He didn't seem to be in any particular hurry, she mused distractedly. That was nice. She'd never needed to talk to anyone so badly before.

"I never knew anyone like Sara. So sweet...so gentle. Her mother died when we were kids, and she came to live with me and my folks. She was the younger sister I never had. I think she knew I'd do anything for her. And she was right.''

Pushing back her chair, Elaine stood, walked to the window, and stared into the city lights below. Her shoulders slumped pathetically as she leaned against the window casing.

"What am I going to do?" she asked the darkness.

Her torment was more than Brent could bear. Standing, he came up behind her and rested a light hand on her shoulder. "You don't have to do anything tonight.''

Elaine closed her eyes for a moment against the soothing tone of his low voice. She felt a fortifying strength radiate from his warm touch and turned to face him. He was standing so close, she could see the gold flecks in the deep green of his eyes. With the exception of the street noises that sifted up to them from the dusky city, they were alone in the silent world of her office.

She found his steady breathing comforting in its rhythm. Ever so slowly, he ran his hand down her arm and twined their fingers together. A thousand unshed tears pricked the backs of her eyes as she tried to swallow the hot lump in her throat. Why was her heart still beating? Surely a heart that was so badly broken could never sustain life.

"I feel like a part of me...died with them," she moaned, her voice low and broken with misery. "I'm so scared. I don't think I'm strong enough to go on living."

Brent's throat tightened painfully, and unable to fight his instincts, he pulled her into his embrace. Her situation struck a particular responsive chord in him. His own mother had gone through a similar ordeal, and he supposed he could understand better than most how she felt.

Bringing her head against his chest, he rocked back and forth and whispered words of comfort. He couldn't be sure how long they'd stood there, locked together by this tidal wave of emotion, when she finally pushed herself out of his embrace.

Smoothing her sleek, shiny, jaw-length hair, and scrubbing at her face with her shredded wad of tissue, she took a deep breath and tried to mask her pain with a watery smile.

"Thanks," she said attempting to effect an airiness she obviously didn't feel. "I...uh...don't usually fall apart like that."

Shades of Elaine the corporate dragon lady were beginning to reappear. Brent recognized this protective wall for what it was and took a respectful step back. Nodding pleasantly, he decided to let her handle what had just happened between them her own way.

"I'm sorry I...uh, took it out on you, there, uh, Clark." Running her fingers through her dark hair, she took a cleansing breath and strode back to her desk on unsteady legs.

He didn't think he'd ever heard her refer to him by his first name.

"No problem," he said, rounding her desk and pulling his satchel out of the chair he'd occupied earlier.

She turned to face him. "Look, I don't usually bare my soul to a mere acquaintance this way." Pink blotches stained her cheeks; her expression was pinched and drawn.

Brent tried to ignore the sting of her verbal slap. This was just her way of keeping him at arm's length ... of coping.

"Um," he nodded blandly.

"And so I'd appreciate it if you kept everything I told you to yourself. I haven't figured out exactly what I'm going to do about...my job and the baby, and whatnot, so until then, please don't say anything to anyone about any of this. Okay?" Her voice carried the clipped tone of an order not to be ignored.

"Sure."

"Good." The word was spoken with breathy relief. Her burst of defiance flagged a little. "Thanks." Removing her coat from the closet, she slipped it over her shoulders.

Brent came up behind her. "If you're ready to go, I'll walk you to your car," he offered, unable to shake the surge of protectiveness he felt, in spite of her prickly attitude.

She seemed to consider his words, then nodded. "All right," she whispered, before she turned out the light and followed him into the night.

"Pssst! Brent! C'mere!" Debbie looked up and down the hallway, before motioning Brent into the employee coffee lounge. Stu and Ray were sitting around a table drinking coffee and shooting the breeze during their Monday morning break.

"What's up?" Brent grinned at Debbie's cloak-and-dagger routine.

Pulling him over to the table, she pushed him into a metal chair and asked, "We just wanted to know ... What's the deal with The Barracuda?"

Brent glanced tentatively around the table at the interested eyes of his co-workers. "What are you talking about?"

"Cut the act, Brent." Debbie slugged him in the arm as she took a seat next to him. "One of the guys saw you walk

Elaine to her car in the station parking lot late Friday night. And—" she narrowed her eyes "—I could hardly believe this, but he says he saw you *hug* her!" She appeared revolted by the very idea.

"That's right, buddy," Stu said, nodding smugly. "You should know better than to try to pull one over on us news hounds," he crowed. "Hey, if you can get the ice maiden to thaw, more power to you, right guys?"

Enthusiastic fist waving and woofing came from the admiring group at the table.

"Yeah, go for it, Brent," Ray advised, giving him the thumbs-up. "Put a smile on her face. For all of our sakes."

Stu drew himself up manfully. "I'd have done it myself, a long time ago, but—" he grinned at his friends "—she scares the hell out of me."

Ribald laughter rocked the break room, and more bawdy comments were made about Brent's apparent virility in the face of danger. It seemed that although everyone found Elaine physically desirable, her managerial style sent fear into the hearts of mere mortal men.

Last week, he'd have found this conversation as amusing as the next guy, but now, knowing what he did about Elaine's situation, it just ticked him off. As much as he wanted to wipe the knowing, self-satisfied looks off the faces of the cozy group at the table with the truth, he couldn't. He'd promised Elaine that he would keep her secret. And, as much as it pained him to let them think the worst about her, a promise was a promise. Brent never went back on his word.

He had a feeling they would sing another tune if they were aware of the selfless act of love their so-called Barracuda had agreed to give to a childless couple. A childless couple that had tragically died only a little over a month ago and left her holding the bag.

"Careful, Brent." Stu assumed the role of relationship mentor. "You being an Iowa farm boy and all, she could chew you up and spit you out. Don't want to lose your job, buddy-boy." He leaned forward and spoke confidentially.

"But, hey. If you manage to get up close and personal with her, try to get us a raise."

The raucous group laughed and beat the table top.

Brent's brow wrinkled in annoyance. He didn't need their unsolicited advice. He was perfectly capable of holding his own with any woman. Even Elaine.

"So, what's the deal? Are you two an item, or what?" Debbie demanded.

Slowly Brent shook his head and took in the wolfish, interested stares of his peers, and was suddenly turned off. Criminy, why hadn't he noticed how obnoxious these characters could be? Thank heavens he was leaving on vacation next week to visit his hometown. He could use a dose of civilization.

"I don't believe you guys." Letting out a weary breath, Brent pushed back his chair and headed, without a backward glance, toward the break room door.

Birds twittered in the perfumed air of the blossoming trees. Spring was literally exploding in a riot of noisy, colorful life around the cemetery. Two gravestones—a stark reminder that she was well and truly alone—marked the final resting place of Robert Johnson, Jr. and his beloved wife Sara. How incongruous it all seemed, Elaine thought morosely, adjusting her sunglasses to better conceal her grief-ravaged eyes.

It was at times like this that Elaine almost wished she had someone to lean on. Someone to share her sorrow with. Someone who understood her pain. Someone like Brent Clark.

She would never forget his kindness the other night. It was his understanding, sympathetic face that had saved her from dying of a broken heart, she was sure.

A gentle breeze teased the unruly wisps of hair around her face and cavorted in a carefree dance through the treetops. It was so unfair. April marched in, burgeoning with life, seeming to mock the solemn block of granite that bore her cousin's name.

What am I going to do? she wondered, virtually filled with despair. She'd always considered herself to be a strong person, but she knew she wasn't strong enough to deal with this incomprehensible situation all by herself. Her two best friends in the world were gone, and she was pregnant—out of wedlock—with their child. A child she'd neither wanted nor planned for. Dear God in heaven, how had this happened to her?

As she stared, bereft and desolate, at her cousin's final resting place, a feeling of Sara's presence—so strong that it caused her to look around—washed over her.

Words, carried to her on the lively spring breezes and whispered in Sara's voice, filled her head.

Be strong, Elaine. Be strong.

Brent poured a cup of Debbie's thick, murky-looking coffee and found himself experiencing a rare moment of blessed solitude in the otherwise chaotic break room. He had missed the station more than he cared to admit these past two weeks. Even though he'd enjoyed visiting with his mother, Margaret, and his friends back in Iowa, Brent was glad to return to the station. After working for WCH for a year, he'd finally earned a vacation, and at his mother's insistence, spent it unwinding on her front porch, eating her home-cooked meals. But, as much as he preferred her mouth-watering pot roast to his usual fast-food fare, there was nothing like sleeping in his own bed in his own apartment.

For some reason, he hadn't gotten a decent night's sleep the entire time he was in Iowa. It could have been the squishy, man-eating mattress on his mother's Hide-A-Bed.... Then again, it could have been the fact that he hadn't been able to get Elaine out of his head. Every evening, just as he'd been about to catch the train to dreamland, her large, haunted, tear-filled eyes had pulled him back to consciousness. He'd spent a good deal of each day, as well, wondering how she was faring.

He'd been tempted to confide in his mother about Elaine's problem, to get a woman's perspective. For who better than Margaret to understand what she must be going through? But he'd thought better of the idea and had respected her privacy even over the miles.

"You're back."

Elaine's cultured voice pulled him out of his reflections and back to the present. He hadn't laid eyes on her since that night in her office, two weeks ago, and he was surprised at how exhausted she looked. Her usually perfect complexion was marred by dark shadows under her eyes, and her cheeks looked sunken and hollow, as though she'd lost some weight.

This couldn't be good. Not for her. Definitely not for the baby. Once again he felt a magnetic wave of protectiveness toward her draw him under its spell.

"How was your vacation?" she asked, moving behind him to the coffeemaker, where she fixed herself a cup of herbal tea.

"Fine, fine. Got a lot of rest," he lied. Yeah. About as much rest as she'd obviously been getting, he thought. If she didn't get some sleep pretty soon, she was going to fall over.

"Good," she said, sighing heavily. "I'm glad you're back. We need to talk about November sweeps. I know it's several months away, but I want to be better prepared than we were last fall. Lately, your pieces have done really well in the ratings, so I'd like you to work on something really special for this coming November."

"Sure." Brent sipped his coffee as he followed her to a table and joined her there. "What did you have in mind?" he asked and covertly watched her cross her legs. For a pregnant lady, she had great ankles. Hell, for a fashion model she had great ankles.

"I don't know. We need something big. Something sensational. We're slipping slightly in the ratings, and if we're going to stay on top, we have to pull a rabbit or two out of the hat." Turning, she pinned him with an uneasy look. "I was thinking about something like your, uh, fire safety series. Those are always popular." She swallowed, as though trying to deal with a bad taste in her mouth. "Only this time, maybe you could tackle accidents in the home. It could be interesting if you visited some emergency rooms and got the story from a 911-type perspective. I don't know...." She toyed absently with her tea bag, her mind obviously not on the conversation at hand. "Gang and homicide stories are always popular. Just be thinking about it, okay?"

"Okay." He nodded, although the fall sweeps were the last thing he wanted to think about. As much as he admired the way Elaine was handling her personal crisis so stoically, he wished she could just forget about work for a while and take some time off to heal.

He sat for a moment and watched her stare off into space, wondering what she was thinking about. Whatever it was, it filled her face with a sadness that he would give anything to be able to erase.

As the break room began to fill with the sack lunch crowd, Brent regretted that their time alone together had come to an end. He felt a certain...camaraderie of sorts with her now, since she'd trusted him with her secret, and he'd wanted to ask her how she was doing both physically and emotionally.

Unfortunately he couldn't do that now. No matter. He'd catch her alone at the next available opportunity.

Later that week, after having abandoned the gang at The Pub, Brent returned to the station and tapped lightly on Elaine's office door. He'd seen the dim light of her solitary lamp glowing forlornly from within and decided there was no time like the present to talk with her. Having no idea how she'd receive another late-night visit, he steeled himself emotionally against her wrath. He'd trumped up a weak reason to be there—that he needed her opinion on a story he was working on.

"Elaine," he called softly and opened her door an inch, "It's me, Brent."

"What is it?" she asked, lifting a wary eye from her paperwork and training it on him.

Waving his copy sheets like a white flag, he entered her private sanctuary and crossed the floor to her desk.

He cleared his throat. "I...uh, just thought I'd get your take on this story I've been working on for November sweeps."

"Oh?" She raised a skeptical eyebrow.

"Yeah," he said offhandedly and tossed the papers on her desk. "I need your approval before I go any further."

"You've got it," she said, pushing the copy back toward him as he settled into one of the chairs in front of her highly polished desk.

"Just like that?" He was surprised. Usually she scrutinized every move he made.

"Just like that." She sighed tiredly.

Too bad she picked now to trust his judgment, he thought, looking at the proposal in dismay. The story he'd proposed was really weak, scratched on a cocktail napkin at The Pub, then pounded out on his computer only moments ago. He was sure that under any other circumstances, she would hate it. It was merely an excuse to see her.

The dark circles still marred the alabaster skin under her beautiful brown eyes. As he took in the subtle signs of her emotional struggle, he wondered how she managed to keep up the high standards of her professional appearance. Although, he guessed, it probably wasn't that hard. She was a natural beauty. She had the kind of gossamer, straight hair that he just knew would be softer than angels' wings to the touch. Not that she would ever let him touch it. No, every inch of her perfect, shapely body screamed "off limits." It was a pity. She reminded him of a priceless art piece kept crated and stored in a collector's closet. What a waste.

Pulling himself back to the business at hand, he said, "Oh...uh, great. Thanks." He picked up his sheets of pathetic copy and, rolling them distractedly, tapped his leg. "So, how are you doing?"

So what if she seemed uncommunicative. What the hell? He was feeling a little reckless. Why not push the envelope?

"I'm fine," she answered primly, in an attempt to stave off any further probing and send him on his way. She was tired, and the curious looks of her staff over the last month had drained her precious reserves.

Brent shook his head, obviously disbelieving. "Really?"

Pulling her lower lip into her mouth, Elaine shook her head. What was it about his down-home, countrified goodness that made her want to throw herself on her office couch and bare her soul? No wonder people found it nearly impossible not to open up to him and tell all. She felt herself melting under his sympathetic gaze, her carefully built facade crumbling.

Had to be her hormones, she reasoned. She was never this easily persuaded to talk.

Setting her pencil down, she slanted her gaze at him, absently taking in his rumpled clothing and disheveled curls. "No. Not really."

"Been rough?"

"Hell." She suddenly found herself basking in the comfort of his nearness.

"I can imagine."

For some reason, she almost believed he could. For some reason, he seemed to understand.

He twisted into a more comfortable position and plowed his fingers through his untamed mop. "Have you given any more thought to what you're going to do about—" he paused, his eyes locking with hers "—the baby?"

She drew an unconscious hand over her still-flat belly. "No. I'm not sure I can keep it."

Leaning forward he asked, "Why not?"

She shrugged. "Because at this point in time, it's overwhelming. And I didn't sign up for this, that's why." She picked up her pencil and rolled it between her fingers as the silence in the room became almost deafening. "Can you imagine me as somebody's mother?"

"Yes."

"Well, I can't," she snapped and tossed the pencil into her desk drawer. "I'm—" hesitating, she cast her eyes guiltily around the room "—considering my options."

"Which are?" Brent tightened his grip on the armrests, and his breathing became shallow. What the hell was wrong with him? he wondered, amazed at his unusual behavior. It was none of his damn business.

"Adoption." Her eyes darted to his.

Agitated, he leapt to his feet and began to pace the room. "Elaine, this baby is all the family you've got left in the world, doesn't that mean anything to you?"

He knew he had no right to talk to her this way, but he couldn't seem to stop himself. It was the strangest thing, but he felt exceedingly protective of the little life she carried. Again, he thought back to his own mother's similar circumstance, and could feel the slender, delicate thread of common experience that had begun to form between them.

"Of course it does," she whispered, nearly as horrified by the option as he was. "What do you think I am? Heartless? But what choice have I got?"

"Certainly not giving it up."

She flushed guiltily at his earnest expression.

"I think you'd be a great mom." His voice lowered to a nearly inaudible level, and he was amazed to find that he actually believed what he was saying to her. "After all, you're a great boss..."

She snorted skeptically and stared at him. "Why do you care what I do?"

Taking a deep breath, Brent rotated his head from side to side and tried to rub the tenseness from between his shoulders. "I don't know." He ambled back to his seat and sank tiredly into its depths. "I guess..." His voice trailed off and his eyes strayed to the window.

"What?" she pressed.

He continued to stare at the bright city lights, as though mesmerized, and began to reminisce.

"My parents were never married, and I was raised by my mother."

Elaine closed her eyes, shook her head slightly and tried to stifle a groan. She could see where he was going with this already.

Seeming not to notice her impatience, Brent continued.
"My mother won't talk much about what happened, but
from what little I've been able to gather, she fell in love with
a wealthy playboy. But, unfortunately for her, she was from
the wrong side of the tracks. By the time she found out she
was pregnant with me, it was too late. My father had bowed
to family pressure and left my mother for a woman from his
social circle, whose name my mother still cannot bring herself to utter." Brent grinned ruefully as his gaze wandered
back to her. "It's true what they say about a woman
scorned."

Elaine arched a delicate eyebrow.

"Mom won't tell me anything about him or his wife, so I
have a pretty limited picture of them. I only know he married someone worse than Satan himself just to keep up his
family's image." A deep dimple appeared in Brent's cheek.
"Mom's a little bitter."

A ghost of a smile tugged at Elaine's lips.

"Anyway, my mother considered putting me up for
adoption. But at the last minute, changed her mind. Instead, she packed our bags and moved us from Chicago
back to Iowa, where she was born. She raised me in the same
small town where she grew up."

A look of longing filled his eyes. "As much as I regret not
growing up in a two-parent household, I guess I really can't
complain. Mom was always there when I needed her. I'll
always be grateful that she had the courage to raise me.
We're still pretty close."

Her troubles momentarily forgotten, Elaine's eyes clung
to him as he shared the situation that was so like her own.
"She sounds like an extraordinary woman."

"She is."

"Whatever happened to your father?"

Brent shook his head. "I don't have a clue, but I'm
guessing he and his wife made a life for themselves somewhere here, in Chicago. Mom won't talk about him."

He could tell he had her interest and leaned forward to
drive home his point.

"The way I see it, our situations are somewhat similar. I was raised by a single woman, who contemplated not keeping me, and hey, I think I turned out okay." His mouth quirked in a rueful grin.

The pensive lines around Elaine's eyes relaxed. "Yes," she murmured, "you did."

They smiled at each other for a moment.

"Elaine," Brent's voice was gentle. "Not all children are lucky enough to be born into the perfect situation. I'm living proof of that."

She abruptly averted her eyes. "But they should be." A defensive veil clouded her face.

"It doesn't always work out that way, though. And a loving environment can make up for a lot."

She stiffened. "What are you trying to say?"

He thought back to his mother's brave choice to have him. "Only that I think you should consider keeping the baby."

She squirmed uncomfortably. "I'm not sure it's such a good idea."

"Why not?"

"Clark, I'm not like your mother."

His eyes swept appreciatively over her chic hairstyle and expensive tailored suit. "No, you're not."

"I made up my mind a long time ago. I have no desire to be a mother. I doubt that I ever will."

"Elaine," he looked her straight in the eye, "why don't you sleep on it some more?"

Sighing in exasperation, she began to tidy the mess on her desk, to show Brent she considered the subject closed.

"Clark, I think I know myself better than you do. And—" he stood and nodded curtly at the door "—I'd like to keep it that way. Good night."

Disappointed, Brent walked slowly to the door. "Good night," he murmured with a smile, before disappearing into the hall.

Chapter Three

"You know, I thought she looked like she was putting on a little weight, but I never dreamed she was *pregnant*." Debbie leaned forward on the break room table, her eyes wide with wonder.

The regular WCH news staff had gathered for their morning break to discuss Elaine's announcement that she was over four months along. Nearly two months had passed since she had confided in Brent, and it had finally become impossible for her to hide the burgeoning truth from her curious staff any longer.

"It was a shock all right," Ray agreed as he refilled his coffee cup before dropping into the vacant chair next to Brent. "Elaine's one of those people you never quite believe is human." He blew thoughtfully into his cup. "The fact that she has a personal life blows my mind."

Brent pretended to stare at the blaring break room TV that was tuned to their station, in a vain attempt to ignore the trite conversation that went on around him. The group at the table reminded him of a pack of vultures circling a fresh kill.

"Man," Stu mumbled around a mouthful of Danish. "Pregnant. Wow."

Yes, Brent decided as he watched everyone buzzing, agog with the deliciousness of Elaine's news, these unfeeling clods needed something else to talk about. In an effort to divert their attention to someone who deserved it, he slipped his foot behind the rear legs of Ray's chair and gave it a quick tug.

Eyes bulging, Ray's arms flailed frantically for balance. He reached for Brent like a drowning man after a life raft, but a final, innocent nudge sent the gangly cameraman backward into a vending machine.

Howls of laughter filled the crowded room as Ray rolled around on the floor and tried to disentangle his long legs from those of the chair.

Debbie rolled her eyes in disgust. "I told you that would happen." She reached for the phone that rang on the wall by her head. "Break room," she shouted into the instrument in an attempt to be heard above the hilarity. "Brent," she called and caught his eye. "It's for you." With narrowed eyes, she mouthed the word *barracuda*.

Brent stepped over the still-prostrate Ray and took the phone. "This is Brent."

The professional, clipped tones of Elaine's voice filled his ear. "My office," she barked. "Now."

"Have a seat." Elaine motioned Brent into one of the chairs situated directly in front of her desk. Her expression was pained as she let her eyes slowly cruise over his attire.

Wiping his hands self-consciously on his blue jeans, Brent crossed the room and took the seat she indicated. He pushed his glasses higher on his nose and wished he'd bothered to tuck in his shirttails before he'd entered the pristine, orderly inner sanctum of Elaine's office.

Something about her cool, tailored appearance always made him feel like such a disheveled hayseed, and that was really beginning to get on his nerves. Dammit anyway, covering the street beat didn't always require pinstripes and wing tips. He'd like to see *her* chase down a story—by showtime, for crying out loud—wearing those impossibly pointy little shoes of hers. She'd be jumping into a pair of sneakers before he could say "fallen arches."

As he sank into his seat, he could tell she was cranking up to nag him about image. Well, he was sick and tired of it. While he was in here, he might as well set her straight on the clothes issue, he thought, noticing her expensive-looking maternity getup. She looked fantastic. But that was her job. He, on the other hand, liked his old corduroys. They were comfortable, and he almost never wore them on the air.

So what if he didn't go for the slick, prissy look of some of his co-workers. So what if he wasn't in touch with his feminine side. In fact, he doubted that he even had one. Big deal. If she thought she could call him in here and rag on him about his appearance again, she could just ...

Brent felt his ill humor dissolve as he watched her battle to maintain the tenuous hold she had on her control. She looked kind of strange. Nervous. Worried. Human.

"I heard the commotion in the break room." The mangled paper clip she twisted between her fingertips betrayed the calm tone of her voice. She sighed, and her shoulders slumped in resignation. "They were talking about my announcement at the staff meeting this morning, weren't they?"

Brent shifted uncomfortably. It wasn't in his nature to lie. However, in light of the circumstances, he decided to hedge away from the entire truth.

"Ray was leaning back in his chair, and the hind legs gave way." He grinned good-naturedly, avoiding her question, thankful that for once it wasn't his apparel that was on the line.

"Oh."

"He's always doing something...like...that..." He could tell she wasn't buying his evasive tactics.

"How did they react?"

"They laughed, but then he deserved it."

Her eyes snapped in exasperation. "To my announcement."

"Surprised." Brent's gaze collided with hers. "They were surprised."

"Surprised," she repeated flatly. "I'm sure they were." She dropped the paper clip and rubbed her throbbing temples, "Clark, I'm well aware of the fact that I'm not very popular around here. You can tell me the truth." She regarded him with hooded eyes.

Maybe, he thought. But she looked so vulnerable sitting there, trying to pretend that she was above caring what anyone thought. Brent could, at that moment, imagine what she must have looked like as a young girl. The plaintive expression on her face moved him.

Once again he was struck by the similarity of her experience, and that of his own mother. Both women struggled with a great deal of grief, both found themselves unprepared for motherhood, both were completely alone in the world.

It was just the kind of predicament that—much to his annoyance—brought out the rescuing tendencies in him.

He knew how hard the loneliness had been on his mother. No one should ever have to go through something like that alone. Not even the cranky, obstinate Elaine. He had a feeling that she still didn't fully realize what lay ahead for her. The physical pain of childbirth, the emotional pain of parting with the baby...

"So, have you decided if you're going to keep the baby?" He winced at his brazen question. What the devil was he trying to do? Knowing he was way out of line, he wondered why was he trying so hard to get himself fired these days.

She sent him a beleaguered look. "Not yet."

"Oh." Brent was crestfallen.

"I'm just taking one day at a time."

Brent nodded. That made sense for now, although eventually she would have to make a decision. In his mind, however, there was no question. Babies were a blessing. Especially this baby. It was probably still too soon for her to see that.

Maybe it was because he'd been raised as an only child, but Brent had always longed for lots of babies of his own. And, as soon as he met a woman who had the right combination of maternal instinct and independence, he'd get himself hitched and get started on that family. Why it should matter so much to him whether or not Elaine wanted to keep her baby escaped him, but it did. Not keeping the baby seemed like a big mistake in light of the fact that she had no other living relatives. For crying in the night, didn't she realize how much a person needed a family?

"Have you got a labor coach?" he heard himself unexpectedly blurting out. Even if she gave the baby up for adoption, she'd still need someone to give her a hand at the hospital. She probably hadn't thought about that yet, he mused, and tried to stifle a grin at the look of shock that stole across her regal features.

She picked up her twisted paper clip and regarded him warily. "A what?"

"A labor coach? Someone to help you breathe?"

She was looking at him as though he'd just stepped off a spaceship.

Feeling the need to breathe a little more deeply himself, Brent fumbled awkwardly with the buttons at his collar. "You know, like they do on TV. Hoo, hoo, hee...hoo, hoo..." He felt stupid.

Elaine blew at her wispy bangs, annoyed. "Clark, I've been breathing without any help for the past thirty-three years. Childbirth can't be that hard, people have been doing it for centuries. Why would I need someone to help me breathe, for heaven's sake?"

He waved his hands in an impatient dismissal of her obvious ignorance on the subject. "Because you will, that's why."

Straightening in her chair, she tossed her silky, dark hair away from her face. "I don't know anyone that I would feel comfortable asking. Besides, I'll be fine by myself."

He couldn't believe that, and felt compelled to set her straight. He hoped his candor wouldn't land him in the unemployment line.

"Yeah, right. Come on, Elaine, surely there must be someone you could ask," he pushed. He hadn't just stumbled out of the cabbage patch. He'd learned a lot about the labor experience the time he'd produced that documentary on childbirth for the independent station back in Iowa. "The Miracle of Life." He'd won a couple of awards for that one.

Labor was hard enough with someone in your court. He couldn't imagine the frightened woman behind the desk—who was trying so hard to be brave—going through such an intense experience without someone there to hold her hand. She obviously hadn't thought this through. She needed his expert advice.

Elaine exhaled noisily. "Clark, as you may or may not have noticed, I spend a great deal of time here at the station. I don't have time for a social life, or... close friends. Since—" pausing, she swallowed "—Sara passed away, I don't have anybody. I'd have to hire someone to coach me, and that's just too humiliating."

"Well, it would be a hell of a lot better than going it alone. I don't think you have any idea what you're in for."

Agitated, she picked up her appointment calendar and snapped it shut. "And you do?"

"I have a little background on the subject. This will probably be the hardest thing you've ever done, and I think you're going to need some help."

Quirking a delicate eyebrow, she stared down her nose at him. "So, why is it, Clark," she asked, settling back into her plush, leather desk chair, "that you happen to know so much about childbirth?"

Brent feigned offense. "You mean you didn't see my award-winning documentary on childbirth? It was a big hit back in Iowa."

She smiled ruefully. "Sorry, I don't get the hayseed channel where I live," she scoffed.

"Too bad. You missed out," he said dismissively, eager to get back to the topic of her own situation. "Elaine..."

"Brent, why don't you just quit while you're ahead, okay?"

The woman could be so hard-headed, he thought, exasperated.

Changing the subject, she picked a file up off her desk and opened it. "Why don't you tell me about that project you're doing for fall sweeps?" she suggested, and looked expectantly at him. "If we're going to win the ratings game we need to get moving on it."

Uh-oh. She was referring to that bogus proposal he'd said he was working on that night in her office. He'd forgotten all about it. In fact, he couldn't even remember the idea. Something about the importance of flossing? Whatever it was, it certainly wouldn't win the ratings game. No. He needed to come up with an award-winning plan. And judging by the increasingly impatient look on Elaine's face, it would seem that he needed to do it now.

Too bad he didn't have another "The Miracle of Life" up his sleeve. His gaze wandered to Elaine's softly rounded midsection. Or did he?

Clearing his throat, he said, "Oh, sure. I thought we could do a series about childbirth. Like "The Miracle of Life" documentary I did in Iowa? It got a lot of critical acclaim. Of course," he cast her a sideways glance, "you'd have to have the hayseed channel to know that."

She frowned. "Miracle of Life?"

"Yes." He leaned forward, suddenly enthusiastic. A wild idea was beginning to form in his head. "It won a bunch of awards, and it's perfect for November sweeps." He feigned innocence. "I thought that's why you approved it."

"I did?"

"Sure did." He reminded her about the night he'd asked for her approval. "You didn't exactly study the copy, but you seemed to think it was a good idea," he said, bluffing.

Elaine squinted skeptically. "Refresh my memory."

"Well..." Brent's mind was racing. It was perfect. He knew that this time around, he could do an even better job on this series than he had in Iowa. He'd learned a lot the first time, and had countless ideas for the new and improved version for the Chicago audience. Talk about ratings. Elaine would have him knighted when he was finished with this piece. And, the best part of all, it would force Elaine to start preparing for the birth of her own baby. However, this would take some pretty tricky footwork to get her to agree.

"Basically we follow a woman and her labor coach through the pregnancy and labor. It's really emotion-packed stuff. The audience eats it up. Nobody can resist a baby. That's why they use them in advertising all the time," he said, improvising. "Babies, puppies and uh... sex are all surefire sales tools."

"Do tell," Elaine said dryly. "And just who were you planning on having play the part of the pregnant woman?"

"I thought we agreed that you would do that."

"What?" she gasped. "No way."

"Oh. Well, in that case I don't see how we can get the thing done in time for November sweeps." He shook his head sadly. "We need to get started right away. It would be so convenient to use you as the talent." Pinching the bridge of his nose, Brent racked his brain for plausible reasons to convince her to play the part. He knew it was the only way she would ever take any help in the form of a birth partner.

"I don't remember agreeing to any such thing," she said suspiciously.

Ignoring her skepticism, Brent decided it was time to pull out the big guns. "Elaine, think of the ratings. Come on. This is a sure thing."

She looked torn, he was pleased to note. He should have known that the way to her heart was through the numbers.

"Okay." She sighed. "I'll buy that." Pulling a pencil from behind her ear, she pointed it at him. "But there's no way I'm going to give birth in front of the Chicago general public."

"I promise, the way I'll do it, no one will ever know it's you."

Tenting her fingers in front of her lips, she attempted to hide the smile she felt threatening. "Just how do you propose to work that little problem out? Have me wear a wig?" As much as she hated herself for giving in to his enthusiasm, she knew he was right. It was a great idea. Having someone to help her over the rough spots when the time came was just an added bonus.

He laughed. He could tell that she liked the idea from an audience standpoint. "No," Shaking his head, he explained his idea. "We'll do it from the mother's perspective. She is the camera, so to speak."

"Brent, I don't want a camera crew in the labor room with me." The thought of the ill-mannered pack down in the break room capturing her *en deshabille* for posterity was just too mortifying to contemplate.

"No problem. We'll set the camera up on a tripod, lock it down and let it roll."

"We?"

"Elaine, somebody has to set up the camera. And—" he went in for the kill "—the way I have it scripted, somebody has to be your labor coach. That's why," he lied, "I was wondering if you picked someone out for that job." Taking advantage of her nonplussed expression, he continued. "But, since you don't have anyone, and since I'll be there with the gear anyway, I should probably just act as coach." He frowned thoughtfully, hoping she would go for it.

Brent held his breath. It was important to him that she have a labor coach, and someday, if he was lucky, he just may figure out why. But for now, he'd just go with his reporter's instinct and rely on the fact that it was good for Elaine and the baby to have a coach. And since nobody seemed to be rushing forward to volunteer, he would just take on the responsibility himself.

All of the women in his documentary had sworn that they never would have gotten through labor without the support of a good coach. After seeing an actual labor, he could see why. It was a painful experience. Elaine had no idea.

Hadn't she been through enough lately without adding a solo labor experience to her list of hardships? Yes, he decided, looking into her large brown eyes. Those eyes that had haunted him day and night since he'd learned of her pregnancy. She'd gotten under his skin. Maybe he could work through it by helping her, he reasoned.

Elaine stared at Brent. "The Miracle of Life" idea had definite appeal. Especially at this stage in her life. Everything he was saying made perfect sense, and she supposed that's what scared her. Good heavens, he wanted to be her labor coach. She hadn't even realized she would need one. Then again, she supposed it would be possible to fill the Library of Congress with all she didn't know about having babies.

She guessed she should be grateful that anyone was interested in coaching her at all. Even if it was only in order to get a story. She tried to quell the wave of loneliness that suddenly settled over her.

In some respects she imagined he had a point. She was definitely not looking forward to labor. Sara had wanted to be with her in the delivery room in the original plan. Her heart twisted painfully at the memory of her young cousin's excitement over the prospect.

It was a moot point now, she thought grimly, looking at Brent's boyish face. His youthful appearance belied the mid-thirties she knew him to be. Something in his gentle expression reminded her of Sara's husband, Bobby. He'd been a cockeyed optimist, too.

What did she have to lose? Nothing it seemed. And she had everything to gain, if Brent knew what he was talking about.

Her response was solemn. "Okay."

"Okay?" Like the sun peeking out from behind a cloud, Brent shot her a disarming grin and beamed at her. "Great. When do we get started?"

Elaine's lips twitched in exasperation. Dammit, how the heck should she know? He was Mr. Miracle of Life. Not her.

"What do you mean, 'get started'? The baby isn't due until October. This is only the end of May. We can get started on the details of this whole thing sometime at the end of summer. Until then, you work on your part of the program, and," she patted her stomach, "I'll work on mine. Sometime around Halloween, I'll call you and we'll go to the hospital and breathe. Okay?" There. That seemed simple enough. Perhaps this wouldn't be so bad after all. She strode around her desk, sank into her seat and considered the matter settled.

It wasn't.

"Ohhh-nooo."

She watched Brent remove and begin to thoughtfully polish his reading glasses. Why on earth did he wear those hideous things? she wondered. Someone should tell him he'd look much better in contacts. Without those nerdy horn-rims, he wasn't that bad looking. Although, she decided, as her eyes dropped to his upper lip, she wasn't much on mustaches.

"What, ohhh-nooo?" she asked, mimicking him.

He grinned. "You can't just march into the labor room and start breathing."

"Why not?"

"Because that's not the way it works. You have to take classes to learn how to breathe. I'll get you a copy of the proposed idea," he told her, knowing that he would be up all night typing. "That will really help you understand why you have to go to birth class."

"Class? You're kidding." Elaine blew impatiently at a wisp of hair that tickled her cheek.

"No. And listen, you'll be glad you took them when the time comes. You'll learn everything you need to know about delivering this baby. Anyway—" he leaned forward enthusiastically, warming to his subject "—you'll need to take a series of classes for about seven or eight weeks and—"

Elaine cut him off. "Seven or eight *weeks?*"

"Sure. Don't worry, I'll be there, too," he said, oblivious to her horror, "gathering information for the series. And I should probably take you to a few of your doctor's appointments as well. You know, so that I can get to know him and anticipate any problems we might have."

Noting her dazed expression, he laughed. "Don't worry, Elaine. We'll only shoot footage of the labor. Tasteful footage," he promised. "The rest of the classes and doctor's appointments are just for background information. We'll leave the camera out of it. It will all come together and be just great, trust me."

Looking into his clear green eyes, she was surprised to realize she did trust him. More than she cared to admit. As he continued with his enthusiastic plans, Elaine, for the first time in weeks, began to feel her spirits rise.

She—of all people—was having a baby. With a country boy cowpuncher as her labor coach, no less. Maybe it would all work out after all.

It certainly couldn't get any worse.

"Mom? It's me." That night Brent went home to his apartment and rooted the phone out from under a pile of laundry. He hadn't talked to his mother in over a week, and after his planning session with Elaine that afternoon, he suddenly had the urge to hear her voice.

"Hi, honey. How's it going?" Margaret Clark's youthful tones carried across the miles, bringing him home to Iowa.

"Fine." He sighed and lifted his feet up onto the stack of newspapers that flowed over his coffee table. "Just wanted to hear your voice."

"That's nice, honey," Margaret sounded skeptical, "but you don't sound fine. What's the matter?"

He never could pull anything over on her maternal radar. "Nothing, really. It's just..."

"Just what?" she pressed.

"Mom, what was it like when you found out you were pregnant with me?"

"Oh, Brent."

He could tell that, as usual, she had no desire to discuss the past. "Humor me, Mom."

"It was such a long time ago. What could it possibly matter to you now?"

"I have a friend in a similar situation, and I need to know."

Margaret was silent so long Brent was beginning to wonder if she'd hung up. "Brent? This friend of yours... You're not the father, are you?"

Brent chuckled at her obvious mortification. "No, Mom. You can relax. I just work with her. Right now she's all alone in the world, and I was wondering how I could help. Thought maybe you could shed some light on the subject."

"It does sound familiar," Margaret mused. "Poor thing. What's the story here? Did the father leave her for another woman?" Her voice was filled with a bitterness that was years old.

Apparently Margaret still hadn't forgiven the evil socialite that had married his father. He knew better than to quiz her about either of them. Nothing would bring their conversation to a screeching halt faster than to ask her anything about his father or his scheming wife.

"No. Nothing like that. It's a long story, but suffice it to say that she has no one but me right now, and maybe it's because of you . . . I don't know, but I want to help."

"You're a sweet man, Brent," Margaret said with obvious pride. "I must have done something right when you were growing up. I would have loved to have had a friend like you when I was in her shoes."

"You would have?"

"Most certainly." Her voice took on the melancholy quality it always did, whenever she allowed herself to travel briefly down the path to the past. "It was probably the loneliest time of my life. I was frightened and ashamed. But," she said, sounding almost amused at the irony of her words, "I had my anger to keep me going. And then, of course, there was you. The sweetest, most adorable little boy in the whole state of Iowa."

Brent's nose wrinkled tolerantly as he pulled his reading glasses off and tossed them on the table. "Mom, please."

"Sorry. Anyway, how is it that you're going to be helping this poor girl?"

He'd never heard Elaine described as a poor girl before. That would most certainly get her undies in a bunch, he thought, grinning to himself.

"I'm going to be her labor coach. You know, support her in the labor room when she delivers the baby. Help her breathe, hold her hand, that kind of thing." He wasn't sure why, but he didn't feel like telling his mom about the series of reports on childbirth they were planning.

"My, my. The times they are a-changin'." Margaret laughed. "Well, good for you. That sounds just fine."

"It does?"

"Sure. It will probably do you some good, too. Get you into the swing of things. You spend far too much time by yourself, since you moved to Chicago." She paused. "Or do you? Have you met anyone and started dating yet?"

Brent hated to disappoint his mother. She was always nagging at him to find some nice girl and settle down and give her a bunch of grandchildren. And, he would like nothing better himself. The trouble was finding someone who fit the bill. There weren't very many single, sharp, independent thinkers who shared his interest in his career—kind of like Elaine, he mused—who also shared his desire to have a big family. Unfortunately, that was where he and Elaine parted viewpoints.

"No, Mom. Not dating anyone. But you'll be the first to know," he teased.

"Oh, sure."

They both knew he'd cut the apron strings when he was still in short pants. Brent never had been a mama's boy, much to Margaret's mutual pride and regret. They chatted for a while longer, catching each other up on their separate lives. Then, after bidding his mother a fond good-night, Brent lay, sprawled out on his couch and drifted off to sleep, dreaming of chubby babies with Elaine's big brown eyes.

"Hi. Come on in." Elaine motioned Brent into her stark, designer-perfect house.

Brent glanced around the sterile interior, wondering where on earth she would ever fit a child among the expensive art pieces and gleaming white carpet.

"Can I get you something to drink? Juice? Mineral water?" Her eyes wandered to his Cubs baseball jersey and faded jeans. "Beer?"

"No, thanks." Brent glanced pointedly at his watch. "We should probably get going. We don't want to keep the doctor waiting...unless you want something?"

"No." Her lips curved ruefully. "My teeth are floating as it is."

They'd taken the warm spring afternoon off to attend Elaine's first ultrasound appointment at twenty weeks, and Dr. Hanson had advised a full bladder for the best possible view of the baby.

Her hands fluttered nervously to her linen blazer, and she tried unsuccessfully to button it. "You don't have to do this," she said, giving him an out. "I can go by myself. I won't mind. Really." She searched his face for signs that he'd changed his mind about doing the story. Part of her almost hoped he would. And part of her was terrified that he would.

Brent smiled warmly. "Of course I do. I'm really looking forward to it." Truth be told, he was more excited about this appointment than he'd been about anything in a long time. A little baby seemed so...refreshing. Especially in light of the depressing news stories he reported day in and day out.

Relief seemed to sweep over her as her button finally found its proper hole. He could see that she was glad he was coming along, although he knew she would never admit it. It went against her grain to depend on anyone for anything. Letting him in on this private experience would take some getting used to for someone like Elaine.

"Okay, then." She took a deep, cleansing breath. "I'm uh—" placing a hand lightly on her swelling abdomen, she stole a glance at him "—a little nervous."

He nodded in understanding and took a step toward her. "You don't have anything to be afraid of. I remember when we shot the documentary, that ultrasound is a piece of cake."

"Oh, I know."

"What is it, then?"

"It's probably silly," she explained, averting her eyes to inspect her spotless carpet, "but I'm worried that he might find something wrong with the baby. I—" she pressed the back of her hand against her pale cheeks in a gesture that spoke of her fear "—don't think I could handle that."

Tiny jolts of joy chased each other down Brent's spine and into his stomach. She was beginning to care about the baby. Would she consider keeping it as well? Maybe there was some hope after all.

"Well, there is always that chance. But it's a small one."
He reached out and tugged on her sleeve. "Try not to worry,
okay?"

"Okay."

"Other than that, how are you feeling?" He didn't like
the look of the dark circles that still shadowed her eyes.

"Fat," she retorted, eyeing her thickening middle.

Brent laughed and threw a companionable arm around
her shoulders. "You don't look fat."

She looked tentatively up into his face. "Really?"

"Really. In fact, you look quite—" He wanted to say
sexy. In his mind there was nothing sexier than a woman
blooming with the life of an unborn child. Especially when
that woman was the already-sexy-as-hell Elaine Lewis.
"—businesslike."

"Thanks." She sighed and turned to inspect his attire. "I
just wish I could say the same for you. Well then, come on,"
she ordered, taking charge in her usual style, "we don't want
to be . . . Oh!" Eyes wide, her hands flew to her stomach.

Brent's heart leapt to his throat. "What?" he barked, fear
filling his gut. "What's wrong?"

"I'm not sure, but I think—" a tiny smile began to tug at
the corners of her mouth "—I just felt the baby move."

A sudden grin split Brent's face. "Are you sure?"

Taking his hand, she guided it to her abdomen and
pressed against it with her own. "You tell me," she murmured, wonder filling her eyes as she gazed up at him. They
both stood silently, barely daring to breathe for fear they'd
miss the tiny signs of life.

And then, like the first, tentative green shoots poking up
from the ashes of a forest fire, they felt it.

"Well," Brent whispered in awe, "I'll be darned."

Chapter Four

"Hey," Brent admonished, as he took in the white-knuckled death grip Elaine had on her handbag, "try to relax, will you? You're about ready to tear the handle off your poor purse."

Smiling apprehensively over at Brent, Elaine made a concerted effort to compose her runaway fears and set her handbag on the floor next to her chair in Dr. Hanson's waiting room.

"You're right," she breathed, willing her pulse to slow. "It's just that I've never done this before, and I'm nervous. I mean, what if he finds some kind of problem? I'm not exactly a kid anymore." Filled with anxiety, her eyes locked with his, seeking reassurance.

Laughing, Brent reached over, took her cold, fragile hand in his large, warm one and gave it a squeeze. "Elaine, no amount of worrying is going to change anything. Lighten up. You're not exactly over the hill—yet," he teased, attempting to distract her.

"Yes, well, I am still your boss, Clark. Remarks like that could get you into trouble." A tiny smile played at her lips.

"Listen," he murmured. "You're going to be just fine."

"Provided my bladder can hold out." She sent him a baleful look. "What's taking so darn long, anyway?"

Glancing over at Dr. Hanson's grumpy receptionist, she smiled insincerely and, lowering her voice, confided in Brent. "I think she does this on purpose. It's a power trip," she griped, thoroughly annoyed at being made to wait.

Brent nodded conspiratorially. "Her eyes do seem a little beady."

Swinging her head toward Brent, Elaine caught him smiling at her in that lazy cowpoke way of his and bristled. He was making fun of her. Although, as much as she hated to admit it, it was good to have him along. Her hand, still clasped tightly in his, drew her eyes, and she could feel his calming presence travel up her arm and begin to work on her frayed nerves.

"I guess that where you come from, out on the farm, having a baby is probably no big deal." As gracefully as she could, she extracted her hand from his.

An easy grin tipped the corners of Brent's mouth.

"But," she said, "to me, it's..." Pausing, she groped for the words to explain how she felt. "It's just that it's a mystery to me. I know that to most women this is a natural, beautiful experience. But I'm not most women." She searched his face for understanding and, thankfully, found it.

"Why don't you just try to think of this appointment as part of the research we're doing for our November sweeps project, instead of a doctor's appointment," he suggested.

"Okay," she sighed, liking that suggestion. Work was something she knew about. "Have you got your note-pad?"

He nodded and tapped his pocket.

"Ms. Lewis? The doctor will see you now." The grand-motherly nurse smiled broadly at them and held open the door that led to the dreaded hallway beyond.

"It's about time," Elaine muttered under her breath, and grabbing her purse, allowed Brent to help her to her feet.

His hand rested comfortingly on her lower back as he guided her to the examining room that the nurse indicated.

"Here we are," she chirped cheerfully and ushered them inside. Picking up Elaine's chart, she waved them into the chairs that were situated against the wall. "Dr. Hanson will be here in a moment, but first I want to find out how we're doing."

"We're bloated and ugly," Elaine sighed, as the nurse slipped the blood pressure cuff over her arm.

Chuckling good-naturedly, the older woman winked at Brent. "They all say that," she said. "But I think pregnancy enhances a woman's beauty."

"Me, too," Brent put in boyishly, leaning forward for a better look at the proceedings.

Eyes twinkling, the nurse noted the reading on Elaine's chart. "Well now, isn't she lucky to have you?" She patted Brent fondly on the shoulder as she motioned for Elaine to hop up on the scale.

Elaine grimaced. It was obvious that Nurse Grandma here was under the misguided impression that they were a couple. And Brent, grinning like an idiot, played the role of proud papa to a tee.

"Good girl," he said to Elaine, when the nurse made positive comments regarding her moderate weight gain and low blood pressure.

She felt her cheeks grow suddenly warm. Never before had one of her staff called her a "good girl." It was clear that she was going to have yet another talk with him. He was carrying this reporter/labor coach thing a bit too far. Although, she decided, as the nurse continued to put her through her medical paces, in some respects it was rather nice.

Still, she didn't want him becoming too emotionally involved. For heaven's sake—*she* didn't want to become too emotionally involved. That's what had landed her in this predicament in the first place. No, getting overly wrapped up in this whole thing would only make it that much harder when it came time to give the baby up. She sighed as a feeling of melancholy overtook her. Why did life have to be so complicated?

"Here you go, honey." The nurse handed her a paper gown. "Take off your clothes and put this on. Dr. Hanson will be here in a moment."

Unfolding the ridiculously small square of tissue, Elaine stared after the retreating woman's back.

"I'm supposed to wear this?" she asked incredulously, holding the crinkly garment up for Brent's amused inspection. "It looks like something I'd use to blot my lips. She must be kidding."

"Better put it on. The doctor will be here any minute," Brent advised, and sitting back in his chair, prepared to enjoy the show.

Clutching the paper to her chest, Elaine vigorously shook her head. "Oh, no. I'm not putting this thing on in front of you." She pointed at the door. "You can wait out there."

Brent snorted, not budging. "For the love of Mike, Elaine. Don't you think your modesty is a bit misplaced, considering what we're going to be doing together in a few months?"

Her fiery cheeks paled. She hadn't thought about the more delicate aspects of this coaching business. How could she gracefully back out of their agreement now? The sudden mental image of giving birth with Brent in the room was extremely disturbing. However, even more disturbing was the fact that she was beginning to rely on his involvement in this experience.

Giving birth in front of one of her employees may not be high on her list of things to do, but then again, neither was going it alone. At least not anymore.

No, she huffed, kicking off her shoes, Brent had gone and made himself indispensable. He had a way of doing that, she noted churlishly, reflecting on his outstanding talents as a reporter.

"Besides," he continued affably, "I'm a farmboy, remember? I've seen it all."

The glint in his eyes told her that he wasn't overly impressed with her silly prudishness.

"Hurry up. Don't want the doc to catch you in the altogether, now, do you?" He pinched the corners of his mouth between his fingers as though trying not to laugh.

Once again, she had the feeling he was poking fun at her. Gritting her teeth, Elaine impatiently shook out the paper gown, unfurling it in his direction. "The least you could do is cover your eyes," she snapped.

"Yes, ma'am," he drawled and tipped the brim of an imaginary cowboy hat at her.

Elaine had no sooner stripped and scuttled into her less than proper attire, when there came a knock at the door.

"Are you decent?" Dr. Hanson called.

Brent snickered.

"Shut up," she groused at Brent, and in a louder voice invited the obstetrician to join them.

Dr. Hanson came into the examination room and grasped Brent's hand in a firm handshake. "I'm so glad that you'll be here for Elaine. This has been a very stressful time for her. Your support means a lot."

Brent nodded. "Just let me know how I can help."

The kindly physician had been extremely sorry to learn of the Johnsons' death and had taken a special interest in Elaine's case.

After the introductions had been made, Dr. Hanson set to work preparing the ultrasound equipment, and then dimmed the overhead lights. Turning the video monitor to give Brent a better view, he instructed Elaine to make herself comfortable on the examination table.

Clutching the sides of the table—as though it might decide to run away with her—Elaine lay back so stiffly that anyone who didn't know better might assume that rigor mortis had set in.

"Try to relax," Dr. Hanson urged, frowning as he began to scan her belly for signs of the baby.

Elaine let go of the breath she'd been holding and glanced uncertainly at Brent. As she tried valiantly not to panic, Brent reached out and pulled a stray wisp of hair away from her lower lip, and then traced its fullness with the pad of his thumb.

"Come on now, honey," he coaxed, scooting his chair up next to her and whispering soothingly in her ear, "take a deep breath."

"I didn't know I'd need you to help me breathe at the ultrasound," she quipped, her voice sounded shaky and feeble even to her own ears.

Squeezing her arm, he chuckled. "See? I told you it would come in handy."

After what seemed like a lifetime, Dr. Hanson finally smiled. "Ah, here were are."

Unable to contain his excitement, Brent leaned forward over Elaine and peered at the video screen. Together they watched in amazement as the outline of what looked like a perfectly formed little spine came into view.

"That's your baby's back," Dr. Hanson informed them, before moving around to show them a set of miniature feet.

Fumbling around in the darkened room, Elaine found Brent's hand and twined her fingers with his. It was well and truly the most miraculous sight she'd ever seen. Her throat constricted tightly with some nameless emotion. Slowly, Dr. Hanson took them on a guided tour of the tiny life, pointing out each incredible new body part as he went.

Brent pointed in fascination at the baby's image. "What are those flashing dots?"

Dr. Hanson paused and pushing a button, magnified the view. "That's the baby's heartbeat. I'll turn on the audio so you can hear it . . ."

Crackling noises filled the room as he adjusted his sound equipment. "There's a lot of static," he commented, searching for the elusive pulse of life. "Probably because you're so nervous."

Elaine tightened her grip on Brent's hand.

"Relax," Brent murmured, squeezing back.

"I'm trying." Her voice was breathy with emotion, as her eyes clung to his. "Really. I'm trying to be calm so I can hear it. But," she whispered, "it's so hard."

Gently Brent smoothed her hair away from her face. "You're doing great," he encouraged.

Elaine closed her eyes and concentrated.

Listen hard, Elaine.

Once more Sara's voice echoed whisper soft in her mind, filling her with an overwhelming sense of peace.

The static on the audio monitor suddenly became rhythmic. Whoosh, whoosh, whoosh, came the delicate cadence.

Slowly opening her eyes, Elaine found Brent watching the image on the screen, his face mirroring her own sense of wonder at the magic of life. Whoosh, whoosh, whoosh. Together, they listened, awestruck. There were no words in the English language that could ever explain the intense poignancy of the moment.

Misty-eyed, Brent smiled at her with incredible tenderness, before leaning down to kiss her gently on the forehead.

Whoosh, whoosh, whoosh. The little heartbeat was strong.

Hear your miracle, Elaine.

Elaine took a ragged breath, as one by one the tears ran down her face.

* * *

"Well, will you look at that?" Stu pointed toward the front entryway of The Pub. All heads at the usual Friday-night table swiveled, following the direction of his finger through the smoggy throng.

There, clutching her small handbag to her chest and looking like a lost child, stood Elaine. Brent felt a tingle of excitement run down his spine at the sight of her. Somehow, in the darkened examination room of Dr. Hanson's office that afternoon, he'd bonded with her—and her baby. It didn't matter to him that the bond was one-sided. Big deal. So she wasn't the bonding type. He glanced around at the tight little clique at the table and decided he liked that about Elaine.

He was delighted to see her.

"What the hell is she doing here?" Ray wanted to know, bringing the front legs of his chair to the floor with a thud.

"Slumming." Dismay tarnished Debbie's gamin features. Huffing noisily, she plucked the paper umbrella from her drink and stuck it in her hair at a saucy angle.

The muscles in Brent's jaw worked in agitation as he listened to their catty comments. Elaine had just as much right to be here as they did. Although why she'd want to subject herself to the inane nightlife of The Pub puzzled him. The smoke, not to mention the lukewarm reception of the WCH staff, should be enough to drive her back to the safety of her office. Especially in her condition.

Catching her eye, he smiled warmly and, much to the chagrin of the folks at his table, beckoned her to join them. Relief seemed to flood through her body as she tentatively returned his smile and began to thread her way through the crowd toward their table.

"Brent," Debbie hissed, under her breath. "What are you doing? We come here to get away from the office, you big goober."

"The party's over," Stu warbled and grinned as Ray began to hum along.

Brent's eyes narrowed threateningly. "Can it," he ordered and, looking back up at Elaine, pulled an extra chair over to the table.

Wound as tightly as a toy soldier, Elaine woodenly approached the gaping group and wondered what in heaven's name she'd been thinking. She didn't belong here. She didn't fit in with these people. Dollars to doughnuts they thought she was out of her mind, and she didn't blame them.

It had seemed like such a good idea back at the office. Friday night had loomed so depressingly ahead of her, and with nothing better to do than go back to her sterile home and feel sorry for herself, she'd decided to take a chance on finding Brent.

Still high from the emotional experience she'd shared with him that afternoon, she got the silly idea that he might want to talk about it. Now she wasn't so sure. Obviously he had his own life—she glanced uneasily at the perky young Debbie's pouty expression—and his own friends.

Brent moved around behind her and offered to help her with her coat.

"Oh, no," she said, suddenly changing her mind about socializing with Brent. "Really, I can't stay." She knew her smile was probably tighter than a pair of control-top panty hose, but she couldn't help it. Her mind reeled, searching for a plausible excuse for showing up uninvited like this. An annoying blush stole from her neck to her cheeks, sending heat all the way to the top of her head.

"Oh, that's too bad," Debbie murmured and nudged Ray with her knee.

Pretending not to notice, Elaine swallowed against her wounded feelings and turned to smile brightly at Brent. "Actually," she said, bluffing, "I wanted to check briefly with you about some questions I had about your November sweeps piece." Her voice trailed off as she ran out of steam. "So, if you have a minute?"

"Sure." Brent sent a departing scowl over his shoulder at Debbie, and followed Elaine toward the door. "You have a question about—?" he started to ask as they reached the street.

"That's okay," she said, interrupting. She didn't have any questions. She just wanted the sidewalk to open up and swallow her whole. "It's nothing that can't wait till Monday. Really." She studied her shoes.

"Oh." He smiled winsomely at her.

"Well . . . I should probably be . . . going." If she hurried, she could probably make it home in time to wash and dry her hair. "I also just wanted to let you know that I'm considering taking your advice."

His brow furrowed in confusion. "Oh?"

"Yes. About, you know, keeping the baby. . ."

Brent's face glowed with surprised pleasure. "You are?" he breathed, quite obviously thrilled at the prospect.

"Thinking about it, yes." She smiled.

"Hey, this calls for a celebration," he crowed, oblivious to the interested stares of passersby. "Let me take you out to dinner."

Elaine's heart hammered against her ribs. "Now?"

"Sure! Why not?" His laughter was giddy.

"What about your friends?" She nodded at the front door of The Pub.

"They're not invited," he said with a grin, and not waiting for her to refuse, hailed a cab.

"You what?"

"I signed us up for a breast-feeding class." Pulling his napkin across his lap, Brent smiled sheepishly at Elaine across the candle-lit table of the small Italian restaurant.

Realizing her jaw was hanging open, Elaine clamped her lips shut and scowled at Brent. "When?"

"Yesterday," he admitted. "It might come in handy for the story. And, I had a feeling you might change your mind about keeping the baby." His smile could light up a ball-park.

"Oh, you did, did you?" Her expression softened. Why not lose herself in his enthusiasm for a moment? she reasoned. Life had been dismal enough lately. Feeling a tiny bubble of joy rise into her throat, she decided to go with the flow tonight. After all, life seemed to go on, whether she wanted it to or not. Might as well try to enjoy it.

"Yeah," he mumbled around a mouthful of antipasto. "I'm really glad. You're going to make a great mom."

"What makes you so sure?"

He stopped chewing and regarded her with solemn eyes. "You remind me of my mother. She's beautiful, bright and tough as nails. Kind of like you."

"I'll take that as a compliment."

"Oh, it is." He winked lazily at her.

Elaine wriggled in her chair. *He thinks I'm beautiful?* The guy really was a cornball. Nobody in their right mind would ever classify her as beautiful. Not with this case of midriff bulge. Why then, under his unfathomable gaze did she suddenly feel so attractive?

Get a grip, she sternly told herself. He probably looked at a new tractor with the same admiration. Still, it was nice to hear a personal compliment. With her social life, they were few and far between.

"So," she said airily, attempting to steer the conversation to safer ground, "you signed us up for a breast-feeding class." Okay, maybe not safer ground. Different ground.

"Umm-hmm." He popped a green olive into his mouth and chewed thoughtfully. "I've been doing some reading about the subject."

Good heavens. She stared at Brent, mystified. He never ceased to amaze her. Why hadn't some nice girl snagged him and given him a batch of children. "You have?"

"Yep. Did you know that on the average, breast-fed babies are eight IQ points higher than bottle-fed babies?" His face was animated as he dug a pamphlet out of his jacket pocket and handed it to her across the table.

"No. I . . . can't say that I did." She stared at the pink paper she held in her hand. "Breast-feeding Made Easy," it read. Elaine rolled her eyes. How hard could it be?

"Well, they are. Plus, it's really healthy, for you and the baby. Don't worry about having to go alone. Birth partners are encouraged to attend. See—" he pointed at the back page "—it's a two-day deal. Pretty neat, huh? We'll learn everything we need to know about feeding little peanut."

"Peanut?" she asked, still stunned that he had taken this on himself. Whatever happened to her resolve to keep him from getting too involved? she wondered absently. Maybe she should tell him no on this thing. Then again, maybe the birth coach was supposed to get somewhat involved. Hell, she didn't know. This was all new to her. At any rate, it probably wouldn't hurt to explore the breast-feeding issue. But a two-day class?

"Two days?" Frowning, Elaine looked up from the etching of the serene Madonna figure happily pressing her babe to her breast. "What on earth could take two days to learn about?"

Brent shrugged. "Lots of stuff. Breast pumps, how to hold the baby, colic, you know, lots of stuff. Come on, it'll be fun."

Elaine sighed. "For you, sure. A class about breasts is bound to be interesting."

Chapter Five

Scrambling like a contestant on a game show, Brent dashed through his apartment, attempting to put it into some semblance of order before Elaine's arrival. Unfortunately, he lamented, as he stopped his whirlwind of activity and stood listening to the incessant ring of his phone, he couldn't remember where he'd stored that particular item. He finally managed to home in on the sound and rescued the poor instrument from under a pile of mail that littered his desk.

"Oh, hi, Mom." Tucking the cordless phone between his shoulder and ear, he opened a desk drawer and shoved great piles of debris inside before squeezing it closed. "What's up?"

"Nothing," Margaret Clark's smiling voice filled his ear. "I just called to say hi. You sound a little out of breath."

"Yeah." Opening the hall closet, Brent kicked his jacket inside and slammed the door before an avalanche of sports paraphernalia could escape. "I'm—" he huffed, picking his coffee table up and tilting it into a waiting wastebasket "—cleaning house. I've got . . . company coming."

"Oh?" Margaret's interest was piqued. "Company."

Brent sighed. He didn't have time to go into it now. "Yeah. Remember? I told you about Elaine Lewis. The producer of the five-o'clock news."

"Ah, yes. The pregnant one."

"The one." Grinning, Brent strode to his kitchen, opened the cabinet under his sink and began loading it with a mountain of dirty dishes.

"Brent, try washing your dishes once in a while, will you?"

He glanced around in amazement. How did she know? She was in Iowa, wasn't she? "Yes, ma'am."

"So, you're having company." Margaret was never easily dissuaded from discussing the possibility of a relationship for her bachelor son. "I take it this friendship is blossoming?"

"Mom, I hate to disappoint you, but I'm just her labor coach." This was true enough, although lately, he'd caught himself daydreaming about Elaine in a most uncoachlike way. Not that he'd ever confide his fantasy life to his mother. "She's going to meet me here any minute now. We are going to our first birthing class."

"Already? How far along is she, anyway?"

Pausing, Brent counted on his fingers. "Let's see. This is August, and she's due the end of October, so...I guess about seven months, more or less."

Margaret hummed thoughtfully. "How is she doing? Last time we spoke, you told me she was finally beginning to recover from the death of her cousin."

"She has her days, but she's working through it." The doorbell rang. "Listen, Mom, she's here. I gotta go."

"Okay, honey. Have fun at birthing class." Margaret chuckled and rang off.

He jammed the antenna back into his phone and raced to the door. Pausing for a quick glance in the hall mirror to check his appearance, he threaded quaking fingers through his unruly curls and tried to get a handle on his emotions.

But it was hard. Ever since the day of the ultrasound, he ceased to be simply a reporter researching a story. Over these past weeks, he'd done his best to remain detached. This was no time to develop a thing for his pregnant boss. Elaine had made it perfectly clear that she had no room in her life for a serious relationship. The fact that she'd decided to keep the baby was a major concession to her usual free-wheeling, workaholic life-style. He knew that for her to make room for a man, as well, would be too much of a stretch. At least at this point.

However, try as he might not to let it bother him, it did. She was going to need some help with this baby. Unfortunately she was just too hard-headed to realize it yet.

Besides, when—and if—the time came for Elaine to go man hunting, it wouldn't be for a guy like him. When she did find time to date, she probably went for those slick-haired yuppie types.

With a momentous effort, Brent managed to swallow the sudden feelings of jealousy that squeezed his heart at the thought of another guy taking his place with Elaine and her baby.

Inhaling deeply, he decided he could wallow in self-pity another day. Right now, he had a birthing class to attend.

"Hi," he breathed, feeling like a teenager in the throes of his first crush as he pulled open his door and invited her into his home. He hoped it looked presentable. He'd never been much of a housekeeper.

"Hi," she answered, entering his apartment and glancing curiously around at his lived-in living room.

Suddenly flustered, Brent closed the front door behind her and, bounding over to his couch, grabbed a newspaper off the cushions. "Here, you should probably sit down."

"Thanks." Following him, Elaine perched awkwardly at the edge of the couch. She smiled nervously up at him. "So. Birth class."

"Yeah. Birth class." He adjusted his reading glasses and glanced at his watch. Claiming the seat next to her, he said,

"We're a little early, still. Can I get you something to drink?"

"Sure."

Brent sprang to his feet and headed to the kitchen.

"Actually," her voice startled him, as she peered over his shoulder into his refrigerator, "I'd prefer some ice cream, if you have it."

The corners of his eyes crinkled in amusement as he glanced back at her. "Ice cream?"

Nodding, Elaine pulled open his freezer. "I can't seem to get enough of the stuff. I never cared about it before, but suddenly it's so...*good.* Any flavor will be— Clark—" she turned and shot him a funny look "—what are your tennis shoes doing in the freezer?"

Damn. How was he supposed to know that she'd go snooping around in his kitchen? Next time, he'd just leave the place a mess. "I like to keep them there. They stay fresher..." he explained hurriedly as he pulled a carton of fudge ripple out of the freezer and slammed it shut before she could discover his sweat socks.

Elaine looked at him skeptically and took a seat at his kitchen table. After he'd loaded up a bowl for each of them, he joined her.

"This should be fun." He winced. Where was the clever repartee he'd rehearsed in front of the mirror all week? Why was he suddenly feeling so shy? Shoot, he'd never worried this much about making an impression on her at work. Maybe he should try remembering that the truth of the matter was, he *was* at work. Elaine viewed his part in this whole thing as nothing more than research, and that was probably how he should view it, too. But it was so hard, he thought, watching her tongue rim the lucky spoon she held in her hand. It sure didn't feel like work. He tightened his grip on his own spoon and began shoveling his ice cream into his mouth.

"Umm." She nodded noncommittally.

They ate in silence for what seemed to Brent like an eternity. Unable to stand it any longer, he racked his brain for something interesting to say. This uncomfortable silence was not what he'd planned as he'd prepared for her visit that afternoon. No, he'd envisioned a far different scenario in which he would amuse her with his snappy, quick-witted humor. And she, for the first time, would begin to see him through different eyes.

"You have the pillows?" Oh well, so much for the witty repartee she probably indulged in with her high-falutin social circle. But heck, anything was better than the silence that threatened to deafen him.

"In the car. Clark—" amusement dimpled her cheeks as she pointed at him with her spoon "—you're not going to ask a bunch of silly questions tonight, are you?"

Silly questions? He stopped eating and looked at her. "What are you talking about?"

"Like you did at the breast-feeding class." She laughed. "I thought I'd die when you asked how I'd feed the baby if I broke both my arms."

"That wasn't such a dumb question," he retorted defensively.

"Okay, then how about when you whipped out your calculator and estimated the per day cost of each breast pump?" She giggled over another large spoonful of fudge ripple.

"You want to be sure you get the most bang for your buck on equipment, Elaine." He glared at her.

Elaine nearly lost her mouthful of ice cream. Eyes dancing with mirth, she leaned forward, teasing him. "Well, when it came to nursing the baby doll with the plastic breast, I have to admit, you had us all beat." She hooted with glee. "Are you going to include that scene in your November sweeps series? The ratings will definitely go through the roof."

"Oh, for crying out loud. Are you done with that?" He pointed at her empty bowl.

"Yep." Still giggling, she pushed her dish over to him and watched in amazement as he bent down and stuffed it under his sink with the rest of his dirty dishes. "Don't tell me," she said dryly, "they stay fresher down there."

Grinning, he crossed the room and pulled her to her feet. "Something like that."

So much for getting her to see him in a new—and improved—light, he thought resignedly. Dropping a companionable arm over her shoulders, he led her to his front door.

Elaine's gaze cruised apprehensively around the eclectic array of parents-to-be that filled the classroom at Chicago Central Hospital. To say that it was an interesting group was to put it mildly. She glanced over at Brent as they took their seats and was suddenly—and exceeding—grateful for his strong, solid presence. She knew Brent was right, that taking these classes was the proper thing to do. She was also aware that it took all kinds to make a world. But, good gracious . . . just what had they gotten themselves into?

Clutching the pillows that the literature had advised they bring, she settled in next to Brent, and wished once again that Sara and Bobby could be here to share in what was, by all accounts, supposed to be an awesome learning experience.

Then again, she decided, scrutinizing the diminutive, aging nurse who strode purposefully to the head of the class, perhaps this experience was more the fearsome variety.

"Hello, everyone, I am Ruby Shocktaag," she barked, "no nonsense" deeply etched into lines on her time-weathered face.

A half a dozen or so expecting couples, including Brent and Elaine, sat in a semicircle facing the chalkboard that hung on the wall up front. After scratching her name in huge letters on the board, the tiny dynamo turned to face the class and smiled rigidly.

"When I call the names," she ordered in her heavy, Latvian accent, "you will tell me you are here, no? Then tell little something about yourself. We must get to know each other, because perhaps I will be with you when you give birth." Snatching a pencil from her tightly coiled bun, Ruby tapped it against her pointed nose and stared with razor-sharp eyes at her clipboard.

Elaine swallowed and blinked at Brent. For heaven's sake, wasn't giving birth scary enough without Nurse Shocktaag and her militant bedside manner? She nervously nibbled her lower lip.

As if reading her mind, Brent smiled reassuringly and took her hand.

Ruby touched the tip of her pencil to her tongue. "Mary and Dick Olsen?"

"Yo," Dick shouted. The balding man grinned Cheshire cat style at the group. Not a large man to begin with, Dick's tan polyester leisure suit appeared to be at least two sizes too big. "I'm Dick, and this is Mary," he bellowed and threw a casual arm around his equally tiny, and terminally shy, wife. "I'm in sales. Cars. This—" he pointed proudly at Mary's middle "—is our first."

Dragging her eyes from the fascinating Mr. Olsen, Elaine darted a quick peek at Brent and unconsciously tightened her grip on his hand. The slight lift at the corner of his mouth was her only indication that he found Dick as unusual as she did.

Ruby's nod was curt. "Vicky and Jason DuShane?"

"Here." Jason DuShane said, his voice cracking, and he promptly turned a brilliant shade of crimson.

Why, he's just a baby himself, Elaine thought sadly, staring at the gangly teen. Maybe her situation wasn't a dream scenario when it came to giving birth, but at least she was old enough to vote.

Shielding her face with her hand, she grimaced covertly at Brent and knew he received and understood her private message. And as much as she wanted to deny it, she was beginning to like his ability to read her innermost thoughts. It was kind of fun to have somebody to gossip with. Somehow it kept her from feeling quite so alone. Although it was almost eerie the way he could tune in to her thought processes.

But then again, any reporter worth his salt should be able to do that, she reasoned, attempting to shrug off the warning bells that sounded in her head. Bells that cautioned her against letting anyone get too close.

"And this is my wife, Vicky," Jason gestured awkwardly toward the homecoming queen at his side, "and this is our first." Giggling, she snapped her gum and thumped Jason's arm in girlish embarrassment. "We're still in school...." He stared at his shoes.

Bobbing her head imperceptibly, Ruby scratched a check mark on her roll sheet. "Liz and Danny Martin?"

Liz smiled placidly at her rotund husband, whose wild hair and beard flowed unfettered over his leather jacket. She tossed her own waist-length hair over her shoulder and raised her hand.

"Here. I'm Liz and this is Danny. We own a motorcycle shop. And this is our first baby, too." Danny's affable grunt could have signaled anything from a casual greeting to a bad case of heartburn.

Elaine nudged Brent with her elbow. Suddenly her unusual predicament seemed almost normal, in light of the interesting cast of characters that made up their birthing class. His answering nudge was playful.

"Brent and Elaine Clark?" Ruby's hawklike eyes scanned the group.

Elaine opened her mouth to speak, but before she could set the authoritative Ruby straight on their marital status, Brent spoke up.

"Here." He smiled genially at the group. "I'm Brent Clark, and this is Elaine. We work for the news department at WCH here in Chicago."

Marking them present, Ruby went on to the next couple.

"Clark," Elaine whispered warningly and pulled his ear down to her mouth, "what are you doing?"

"What's wrong?" he whispered back.

For someone so in tune with her every thought, he could certainly be obtuse. "They think I'm having your baby," she snapped, scandalized.

"Big deal." His brow knit in annoyance.

Grabbing a handful of his midnight curls, she tugged his ear back to her lips. "It *is* a big deal. You're a local celebrity... kind of. What happens when word gets out that I'm having your baby?" Good heavens. He hadn't even kissed her yet.

Yet? Where had that come from?

"Fine." He sighed in exasperation. "As soon as she's done, I'll explain that you're a surrogate mother, and I'm a reporter here to gather information for a show we're doing."

Okay, she thought, loosening her hold on his earlobe and looking around the room. So he had a point. No use going into detail about their particular circumstances. Pursing her lips she squinted at him through narrowed eyes.

He grinned and much to her dismay—and pleasure—kissed the tip of her nose with all the indulgence of a typical father-to-be.

Elaine squirmed uncomfortably. She really shouldn't enjoy his company so darn much. It's just that his neophyte charm had a way of getting under her skin.

He really was a good guy, she mused, comparing him to the other male members of the group. Compared to Brent they were all pretty lame. Personally she couldn't envision herself married to any of these oddballs, let alone giving the world an oddball junior. No, she decided as she counted the gold chains that ornamented Dick's furry chest, she was definitely the luckiest woman in the room.

Suddenly realizing that she'd been woolgathering for quite a while, Elaine hoped that Brent had been paying attention and tried to catch up with the lessons that had gone on without her.

"...and breathing is of utmost importance," Ruby announced. "With pillows you bring to class, take seats on floor."

Brent shot Elaine an I-told-you-breathing-was-important look, as he helped her out of her chair and onto the pillows she'd brought along.

Following their tiny dictator's instruction, Elaine leaned back against Brent and tucked the pillows under her legs. She could only hope, as he rested his hands comfortably around her blossoming waist, that he couldn't feel the resounding thunder of her heartbeat. What came so naturally to every other couple in the room seemed exceedingly intimate to Elaine. She could feel his breath tickling the back of her neck. He was so warm, she noted, settling gingerly into position. And so soft. No, hard really. Hard and soft. And warm. She hated herself for noticing how wonderful, and how right, it felt to recline into his embrace. It had been so long since she'd been held.

Nurse Shocktaag marched to the middle of the floor and crouched into a ball.

"I am the contraction," she thundered and slowly returned to an upright position. "Come now. Breathe with me." Jerking her body back into a ball, she puckered her thin lips and began to exhale. "Contraction is beginning now! Hoo, hoo, hee!"

"See?" Brent arched a superior brow.

"Yeah, yeah, yeah." Elaine rolled her eyes.

Ruby looked at them sternly. "Mr. and Mrs. Clark! No time for talking. Hoo, hoo, hee." She made the words sound like firing bullets.

After what seemed to Elaine like an inordinate amount of practice, the class finally mastered the art of hoo-hoo-heeing and moved on to hee-ha-hoo and an assortment of other varied and uninteresting breathing patterns.

Then, as part of that evening's grand finale, Ruby ordered everyone back into their seats and turned to face her class.

"Now we will get to know each other a little bit. We will go around to see what each man thinks of becoming Daddy, and why he is taking class with Mama," she announced. "Jason, you will begin," Nurse Shocktaag informed the red-faced teen.

Elaine's head snapped up. Oh dear, she thought wildly, what were they going to do? Brent wasn't becoming Daddy. He was just along for the ride. Maybe they should leave. She scanned the room for the nearest and most unobtrusive exit.

All eyes in the room focused on the visibly shaken Jason.

"I'm...uh," he squeaked, "mostly scared. But then, I don't have much to go by." His youthful voice carried the weight of the world. "My old man split when I was just a kid." He paused and glanced at his young bride. "I'm here to learn how to help Vicky. I guess I'll just try to do my best."

"Good." Nurse Ruby nodded. "Dick?"

The bantamweight car salesman sat up straight in his chair, his chain-link chest expanding pridefully. "I'm attending because Mary here twisted my arm." Dick chortled gleefully, enjoying his own peculiar brand of humor.

"All kidding aside—" his thoughtful frown was practiced "—I think having a kid will be a giant kick in the head. Can't wait to meet the little beggar. But to tell the truth, I'd rather sit in the waiting room when the time comes and let Mary here do her thing. But, hey, if she needs me, I'm there. Know what I mean?" His brash laughter filled the silent room.

Ruby scowled. "Okay. Danny?"

Danny grunted and adjusted his leather jacket over the Grateful Dead insignia on his T-shirt.

"Uh, I'm here to try to convince Liz that we don't want to try this at home. She has it in her head that a hospital would give the kid bad karma or something. Also, I think she should go for the drugs." His bushy beard twitched in amusement. "Hell, I would."

"Thank you, Danny." The muscles in Ruby's jaw jumped spastically as she swung to face Brent. "Brent?"

Closing her eyes tightly, Elaine braced herself for whatever her pseudohusband might get it in his head to say.

Brent let his gaze wander slowly around the room, a soft smile adorning his gentle face. Leaning forward he braced his elbows on his knees and pulled Elaine's hand into his lap.

"I think that being there to welcome a tiny new life into the world," he began, "will probably be the most powerful, humbling experience I'll ever have. It's such a mystery...I seriously doubt that there is anything on this earth that will compare to the feeling of holding a newborn child in my arms for the first time." He spoke in a tone filled with awe and respect.

"To me, being a father figure means being there. To help mend broken hearts and to help make dreams come true. To hold and comfort them when they're scared of the dark." His expression was sympathetic as he looked over at Jason. "Never leaving."

Tears brimmed into Elaine's eyes, and she felt her throat suddenly fill with a hot lump. Sara would have loved him.

Brent sighed, his honest expression filled with the hope of his small-town upbringing. "In my line of work, I see so much sorrow and despair. But the way I look at it, babies, so pure and innocent, are a gift from heaven. It's like... everything is shiny and new. I don't know," he shook his head and smiled at Elaine, "they give me hope. I wouldn't miss this for anything. I'm here to support Elaine. And when the time comes, to be there for the baby."

Ruby Shocktaag's face relaxed into a soft smile for the first time in probably fifty years.

"Thank you, Daddy," she whispered, before moving on.

"Stop it!" Elaine squealed, wiping the tears of mirth that streamed down her cheeks. "I mean it, if you don't quit, I'm going to have this baby right here in your car."

Brent pulled his car to a stop near the spot where Elaine's Jaguar was parked in front of his apartment. Jumping out, he rounded his vehicle and, pulling open his passenger door, helped Elaine—still laughing helplessly—to her feet.

"Hey, Shecky, get the jet. I'm outta here!" he yodeled, continuing his impression of the flamboyant Dick Olsen as he took her by the elbow and walked with her to her car. It was a mild summer evening, and the scent of newly mown lawns and flower blossoms followed them through the twilight to her waiting Jaguar. He stood patiently while she tried to pull herself together enough to locate her keys.

"Yes, no, yes, yes, no," he muttered under his breath, as she dissolved into laughter, abandoning the search through her purse. He was feeling buoyant, not just from the birth class experience they'd just shared, but from the easy camaraderie they'd fallen into on the way home. The atypical mothers- and fathers-to-be, provided an endless source of fodder for making Elaine laugh. He loved her deep, throaty laugh. It was sexy as hell.

Giggling, Elaine hiccuped. "Would you just *stop?*"

"Yes, no, yes, yes, no." Brent grinned and grabbed her purse out of her hands. At the rate she was going, they'd be out here in the parking lot all night. "Don't mind me, I'm just..."

"Matching you to a car!" they both crowed in unison, then fell against each other in paroxysms of laughter.

"What on earth was that man talking about?" Elaine referred once again to the tiny car salesman with the big voice, her eyes dancing up into Brent's.

He looked down into her relaxed expression and was once again struck by how beautiful she could be. It had been a long time since he'd seen her smile like this. "I don't know, but half the time I got the feeling he was communicating with another world." Brent fished the keys out of her purse and handed them to her.

Taking her purse from him, she looped its handle over her shoulder and leaned back against her car. "Can you believe he's going to be that poor kid's dad?" She ran her ignition key over her full lower lip.

Unable to stop, Brent found himself staring, mesmerized, at the thoughtful gesture. "Almost makes me grateful for my fatherless childhood," he murmured teasingly.

"You know, the sad thing is, he wasn't the nuttiest guy in the bunch, either." Elaine caressed her tummy with a protective hand.

"True, but at least he seems to care."

"Yes," she admitted, "he does seem to care."

Not wanting the evening to end, but at the same time unsure about inviting her in for coffee, Brent racked his brain for ways to keep her from going home. "How about that couple, what was their name? The ones that dressed exactly alike?"

Her merriment rippled through the fresh summer air. "The Harlows? I thought they looked cute."

"Oh, sure. Come on, they looked like pigs in a blanket and you know it."

"Brent!" Elaine gasped with surprise.

His face flushed with pleasure. He wondered if she realized she'd called him by his first name. "Well, really, Elaine. When you wear matching brown sweatsuits at this stage of the game, you're asking for trouble. Can you imagine us dressing exactly alike?" His observant gaze roamed over her lush figure.

"Well, no, not exactly, but you haven't got Mr. Harlow's beer belly, either." She returned his bold inspection, letting her eyes flick over his trim waist and narrow hips. "Actually," she teased, "I think you'd look good in something like Dick wore tonight."

"Ha. I may have terrible taste in clothes, but even I'm not that bad."

"No," she agreed. "You're not." Her eyes drifted up to his. "Not bad at all."

"You're not so bad yourself, little Mama."

"You think?" she asked, and he could feel her need for his reassurance. The kind of reassurance that only a man can give a woman.

"Mmm. Not bad at all."

He reached up, as she leaned back against her car, and traced her jaw with his fingertips. He loved this vulnerable side of her personality. It was a side that she so seldom let steal to the surface of her corporate persona.

"Thanks," she whispered up at him. Twining her fingers with his, she captured them in a gentle squeeze between her cheek and shoulder. "And, thanks for going with me tonight."

"I wouldn't have missed it for the world," he said and knew that it was true. Wild horses couldn't have kept him away. And unfortunately it was beginning to feel as though those same wild horses couldn't keep him from making a colossal fool of himself right now. Because it was at that moment he knew he had to kiss Elaine or die trying.

To hell with the fact that she was his boss. His pregnant boss, at that. And to hell with the fact that she fancied him to be nothing more than a hick from the sticks. There had been far too much happening between them. He needed a physical outlet for the connection he felt with her. Hoping against hope that she would understand, or at the very least let him keep his job, he rested a palm on the roof of her car and lowered his mouth to hers.

Chapter Six

Elaine could scarcely believe that she was allowing one of her reporters to kiss her good-night, let alone the fact that she was enjoying it so...immensely. She was seven months pregnant, for heaven's sake. She had no business enjoying herself this way.

And with Brent Clark, of all people. What on earth was the world coming to, she thought fuzzily, loving the feel of his mustache as it tickled her upper lip. Closing her eyes against the hazy fog that swirled around her dizzily spinning head, she clutched his well-muscled upper arms and leaned into him for support.

"Lordy, Lordy," she whispered against his warm, supple mouth. The man sure could kiss. Merciful heavens, he must have put in a few very heavy practice sessions with some neighbor girl or another out behind the barn.

"Pardon?" Brent breathed raggedly, as he briefly tore his lips from hers only long enough to rain kisses down her jawline and across her chin.

"Nothing," she managed to answer, just before he claimed her mouth again.

What was happening here? She tried to analyze the situation, but it was hopeless. She was hopeless. Hopelessly caught up in the moment. Sliding her hands over his tightly corded shoulders, she twisted her fingers together and locked them behind his strong neck. Funny, she'd never noticed how...large, he was before. Even in her present condition, he made her feel almost petite. She'd always thought of him as being much smaller. An underling.

So much for that theory, she mused, nearly drunk with her need for his touch. It had been so long since she'd been touched, she supposed it could be possible that her tastes in men had changed—but really—*Brent Clark?* New kid on the WCH block, she thought, angling her head to give Brent better access to her mouth.

She would definitely have to give this some thought. Later. When she could think straight. Not now. The mind-numbing desire that had somehow become a roaring backdraft between them, made any kind of rational thought completely impossible.

She clung to Brent as her legs turned to Jell-O beneath her, and savored the warm, sweet taste of his kiss. It was so exquisite. How could this be? Her head was reeling. Obviously she needed professional help. Yes. Counseling to discover why, in less than one short year, she'd managed to sabotage her upwardly mobile, fast-track-to-success life with a baby and this...this...labor coach. However, when she factored in the thrill she was getting from kissing him, it almost didn't seem like such a raw deal. Maybe the upwardly mobile, fast track wasn't all it was cracked up to be.

"Elaine?"

The husky word was sharp and hot in her ear.

Who was Elaine? Ahhh, yes. She was. Of course.

"Yes?" Letting her head fall back, she breathed her question and gazed up at Brent through the half-open slits of her eyelids.

Brent pulled her hands from around his neck and clasped them firmly in front of his body. "You should probably be on your way. It's getting late..."

He had a very strange look on his face.

Groaning inwardly, Elaine felt the heat of a thousand white-hot suns burn her cheeks. How mortifying. She, Elaine Lewis—much-sought-after, hotshot Chicago news producer—was being sent home.

And why not? What man in his right mind, even a gentleman like Clark, would want a disagreeable unwed mother, complete with water-retention problems, throwing herself at him? She was supposed to be helping him research a story, not jumping his bones in the parking lot of an apartment complex. She could just die. What on earth had possessed her to allow this to happen? *Ohhhh.* Why didn't someone just shoot her and put her out of her misery?

She tried to swallow past the sudden dryness in her mouth.

"Of course. You're right." Smiling weakly, she fumbled with her car keys in the uncomfortably confining space between Brent and her car. Why did he have to stand so damn close? Especially since he was in such a hurry to get rid of her. After several unsuccessful attempts, she was finally able to unlock her door and slip into the cool, leather interior of the Jaguar.

Gunning the engine, she rolled her window down, and avoiding Brent's eyes said, "Thanks, Clark. It was a great class."

Too humiliated to wait for his response, she backed out of her parking spot and roared off into the sunset.

Later that night Brent lay in his bed, filled with angst, tossing and turning and waiting for that elusive train to dreamland. But it was a fool's errand. No way in hell was he going to get a lick of sleep. Not after the stunt he'd pulled earlier with Elaine.

What an idiot! What in heaven's name had convinced him that kissing his boss would be a good idea? Especially since it had taken him so long to gain her trust both as a reporter and a labor coach. Thank God he'd at least come to his senses long enough to send her on her way, before he did something really stupid that she'd never be able to forgive him for.

All he could do now, he decided as he quite literally punched the stuffing out of his pillow, was pray that his error in judgment hadn't killed their fragile bond of trust.

Exhaling in misery, he flopped over onto his back and stared, unseeing, through the darkness at the shadows on his ceiling. He'd always prided himself on his ability to stay objective in any situation. It was part of what made him so good at his job. Why then, had he thrown caution to the wind and come on to Elaine the way he had?

And, why did it have to be so damn good?

Of course, once he'd finally come to his senses—before he took her right then and there out in the parking lot— she'd taken off like a bat out of hell. Couldn't wait to get away from his clumsy, unsophisticated advances. Probably went home to call her lawyer and see about slapping him with a sexual harassment suit.

"Ohhh man," he groaned and pulled his pillow up over his face.

Gosh darn it anyway, it had been such a nice evening, too. Before he'd gone and messed it up. All through birthing class he could almost imagine that he and Elaine were married. He felt the most mysterious connection with her. Almost as if it were his baby she was carrying. The mere thought made the blood run hot through his body.

No. He'd never get to sleep tonight. Wouldn't the guys at the station have a field day over this? He groaned again and pounded his forehead with his fist until his ears began to ring. And ring.

He stopped hitting his head and listened. Fumbling in the dark, he reached for, and finally found, his phone.

"Hello?" His heart pounded the way it did every time his phone rang this late at night. It was usually always the station. It was usually always bad news.

"Clark?"

It was Elaine. Her voice sounded shaky. This was it. She was calling him to chew him out.

"Yes..."

"I hate to bother you this late at night, but something's wrong."

Brent cringed as he sucked his lower lip into his mouth. Yep. She was going to tell him that they could no longer work together after he'd mauled her the way he had down in the parking lot earlier.

"And," she continued in the same quavering voice, "I didn't know who else to call."

What was she talking about? Surely if she was going to read him the riot act, she'd dialed the right number.

She moaned slightly, breathing heavily into the phone. "Clark, I think I'm in labor."

Brent suddenly found himself standing next to his bed, as though some giant puppeteer had yanked him to his feet. Labor? It couldn't be. It was too early. "Are you sure?" Using his best reporter's voice, he tried to keep his panic from showing. It was far too early. She was only seven months along.

"Clark," she cried in exasperation. "How should I know? I've never done this before. I'm having regular contractions, and—" her voice dropped to a frightened whisper "—I'm scared."

Pulling his jeans on over his pajama bottoms, Brent hopped around his bed and searched for his shirt and shoes. "Stay where you are," he barked, feeling his pants pockets for his car keys. "I'll be right there."

"But I don't want to stay in bed. This is ridiculous. I feel just fine." Elaine sighed as she flopped back on her pillows and watched Brent fold her large, fluffy, white comforter.

He tossed it onto the pine chest that stood at the foot of her four-poster bed and, turning to her, yawned broadly.

"Good. I'm glad you feel fine. But you heard Dr. Hanson. He wants you to stay in bed for the rest of your pregnancy, or you could lose the baby." Lifting his arms up loosely above his shoulders, he stretched and rotated his head. "You're lucky he didn't make you stay at the hospital tonight. High blood pressure is nothing to fool around with, Elaine. You don't want to have the baby now," he said as he pinched the muscles in his neck.

He looked tired, she noted. It was no small wonder, considering it must be after three in the morning. Glancing at her bedside clock, she saw she was right.

"But I have work to do," she moaned petulantly. "Tons of work. I simply can't stay in bed. And what about our story for November sweeps?"

Brent snorted. "Elaine, to hell with the sweeps story. As far as I'm concerned, we can do something else. The life of your unborn child is far more important than any stupid news story. Give it a rest, okay?" His expression was haggard. "I'm sure the station will get along just fine without you for a while."

Twisting her freshly laundered sheets into a mangled ball, Elaine tried to stem the tears she felt welling to the surface. Damn her hormones. Would she never be free of these impossible mood swings?

Seeming to read her distress, Brent's face softened. "Okay, maybe we won't get along just fine, exactly, but we'll muddle through. Hey, give us some credit. We've probably learned a thing or two from watching you."

"You're just saying that." She could feel one lone tear blaze a trail down her cheek.

Brent settled next to her on the edge of her bed and reached out to tuck an errant strand of hair behind her ear. Then, extracting the crumpled ball of her sheet from her hand, he gently touched it to her damp cheek. "Oh, honey. Listen. We'll find a way to win the ratings game," he reas-

sured her, misunderstanding the reason for her depression.
"Until then, you just need to take it easy."

She didn't give a damn about the ratings anymore. She
only wanted to make sure that he would still be her birth
partner. Her doctor's appointment partner. Her birth class
partner. Her partner. "Brent?"

"Hmm?"

"I know that you—" feeling silly and emotional, she
sniffed and reached over to her nightstand for a tissue
"—probably have better things to do with your time, now
that we won't be working on our project together, so I understand if you—" she swallowed, the tears beginning to
flow in earnest now "—you know, don't want to...uh,
coach me, now...."

Brent reached over and gathered her into his arms.
"Sweetheart, if you're trying to get rid of me, you can forget it. I'm coaching you and that's final, got it?"

Sighing raggedly, she whispered, "Got it."

He had far too much time invested in this project to call
it quits now.

That was a lie.

He had far too much emotion invested in Elaine to call it
quits now.

But he couldn't tell her that. Swaying slightly, he rocked
her to and fro as she slumped tiredly against him. She must
weigh no more than a feather, baby and all, he mused, enjoying her body warmth as it seeped through his shirt. He
planted a few kisses into the fragrant tresses at the top of her
head. She smelled of lilacs. He loved the smell of lilacs. It
reminded him of springtime back home.

Elaine closed her eyes and enjoyed the hypnotic rhythm
of his relaxing movement. She could feel Brent's cheek lift
slightly as he smiled against the top of her head.

It seemed so right, having him there at three in the morning. How strange. Never before had she allowed anyone to
see her this way—tired, frightened, bloated. She must look
a perfect wreck.

Then again, when had what she looked like in front of Brent become so important? That was one question she didn't want to face. Because the answer—since he'd kissed her earlier—was mind-boggling. Especially at this hour. She was still reeling from the potency of that kiss. And from the humiliation.

It had been sheer, unadulterated terror that had prompted her to dial his number and ask for his help. Because just as she'd vowed that she was never going to let him get that close to her again, the pains had started. He, unfortunately, was the only person in the entire world she could think of to call. Sweet, dependable, salt-of-the-earth Brent.

How pathetic that he was the only person that had come to mind. Really, she thought tiredly, as soon as she was able, she was going to have to do something to remedy this situation. Cultivate some new relationships. Go out on a date or two.

Elaine stifled a yawn against Brent's steadily beating heart. Oh, um humm, right. She was going to start dating with an infant on her hands. Life. She smothered another yawn. Sometimes it was just so unfair.

Brent's voice rumbled comfortingly in her ear as he spoke. "You know," he said, the stubble from the day's growth on his jaw made an interesting sound as it rubbed against her hair, "I was really scared when you called and said you were in labor."

"You were?" Elaine lifted her cheek off his chest and looked up into his eyes. They were such nice eyes, really, when he wasn't wearing those dopey glasses. "Why?"

The tiny hairs at the side of her face stirred as he huffed. "Because I'm concerned about you. And the baby."

"You are?" She eyed him speculatively. Why should he care? Good heavens, even on her best day at work, she was nothing but a pain in his side. Her expectations were always higher of him than of the rest of the crew. She rode him, because she knew he could take it. Because he was better than they were. No, her constant harping certainly couldn't have endeared her to him, could it?

"Yes." There was a quiet emphasis on the word.

His gaze lowered, as did his voice, and Elaine felt the same fire that had flashed between them that afternoon begin to spark. Oh no. She'd promised herself that she wouldn't let this happen again. Why then, did she feel herself once more beginning to melt under those unfathomable, sea green eyes of his? He shifted his position slightly, and suddenly, she found herself half lying across his lap.

"Why?" she breathed, hoping against hope that she was more than just a story to him.

He shook his head and inhaled deeply. "I'm really not exactly sure. Lots of reasons, I guess. And no reason at all. It's a mystery."

She nodded, trying to understand.

"Elaine?" His lips hovered a hair's breadth above hers.

"Hmm?" She felt so delightfully warm and wonderful.

"I really think—" he sighed heavily and, moaning, shifted her off his lap "—that I should be going home. Because the way I'm feeling, if I don't leave right now, I'll be here all night."

Her stomach tightened. Of course. He had to leave. He must be exhausted. How thoughtless of her. Flames of humiliation licked her cheeks. She was really batting a thousand with him today.

"Sure. Go. Go." Smiling brightly, she shooed him toward the door. "I'll be fine."

"Good. But, if anything, and I mean *anything,* should happen, I want you to call me immediately. Okay?"

"Okay."

"Well, then." He paused at her bedroom door and smiled down at her. "Don't get up," he teased, "I can find my way out."

Surely her face would crack from the effort it took to smile so cheerfully. "Okay," she chirped again.

"I'll call you in the morning," he promised.

Elaine listened as he locked and closed her front door. "Okay," she whispered and, burying her face in her pillow, suddenly felt lonelier than she'd ever felt in her life.

"What have you got?"

"Chinese."

"No," Elaine huffed, cranky, frustrated and bored out of her gourd. "Not the food." She pointed to the pile of folders Brent balanced under his arm, along with the bag that was emitting the most enticing smells of ginger and sweet-and-sour sauce. "Those."

Brent dropped his load on what had become "his side" of her bed. During the two months since Elaine had been confined to bed, he'd taken to bringing her dinner, magazines and assorted toys to amuse her, and bits and pieces of work that the higher-ups at the station felt she could handle from her home. He would spread the food, picnic-style over her covers, and they would spend a companionable hour or two together before he headed home to his place.

"Debbie sent these." He pushed the files in her direction. "Says they need your signature. Also, Stu wanted you to take a look at a story proposal he's hot to do on some women's wrestling team. Thought it might be a good one for November sweeps." He dug through the bag of food and tossed her a pair of chopsticks.

Elaine sent him a baleful look. "Sounds like his kind of story," she sighed. "Not exactly what I had in mind to win the ratings war, though."

"Brent laughed. "Oh well. He also said something about wanting to go undercover to expose them, or something like that. It's all in there." He gestured to the pile of work with his own chopsticks. "Hope you feel like Szechwan."

"I feel like a beached whale," she said crabbily. "But, Szechwan will be fine."

Brent smiled indulgently and handed her a carton of rice and a paper plate. "You're in a good mood. Maybe we should talk to Stu about getting you on that wrestling team."

That made Elaine grin. "Well, for crying out loud, I want to get out of bed. I feel fine. I really don't see what difference it would make, considering I'm due next week, anyway."

Brent stopped eating and stared at her. "Already?" Was it the end of October? How could that be? He wasn't ready. Even though Dr. Hanson had okayed their weekly attendance at birthing class, he still wasn't sure he'd learned everything he needed to know to help Elaine get through labor.

"Yes," she mumbled around a mouthful of sesame beef, and then, suddenly remembering her news, her eyes lit up. "Oh! Guess who called!"

Shrugging, Brent scraped the rest of the cashew chicken out of the carton and onto his plate. He'd gained at least ten pounds since Elaine had gotten pregnant. He almost couldn't fit into those old high school corduroys of his. "I give."

"Liz Martin. She says Dick and Mary Olsen had their baby yesterday."

"Really?" Leaning forward, he grinned, eager for her news.

"Yes," Elaine crowed, bouncing up and down on the mattress. "And you'll never guess what! He fainted!" She screamed with glee.

"He did?" Brent breathed, his eyes wide with wonder. "Man. I sure as hell hope I don't do that."

Shaking her head with a confidence he was nowhere near feeling, Elaine said, "Oh, you won't."

"What makes you so sure?" He looked at her, curious.

"Because you're not a little wimp like Dick."

He wasn't? Of course, *he* knew that, but Elaine? Well, he couldn't ever really be sure exactly what she thought of him as a man. She was always so busy bossing him around as an employee. And as her assistant in this pregnancy.

"I'm not?" he asked dryly.

"No," she regarded him thoughtfully for a moment. "You're made of much sturdier stuff."

Not entirely dying to know what "sturdier stuff" was composed of, Brent asked, "What'd they have?"

"A boy. Richard Olsen, Jr. Five pounds even and eighteen inches long. Must take after his folks," she mused.

Brent shook his head and smiled broadly at Elaine. It was happening. The babies were beginning to come. "In the immortal words of Dick Olsen—Shecky, get the jet," he roared, in a tribute of sorts to the new father, and they laughed together, sharing their private joke.

"Do you want me to call 911 now, or would you rather I wait until you keel over?" Brent asked churlishly, eyeing with disgust the jelly doughnut Ray was dipping into his coffee cup.

"What's the bee in your boxers?" Ray's eyes narrowed defensively before he stuffed the soggy confection into his mouth. "You've been a bear all week," he mumbled, and looked across the break room table at Stu and Debbie who were nodding in agreement.

Brent shrugged impatiently and checked the battery in his pager for the umpteenth time. Ray was right. He'd been jumpier than a cat in a roomful of rocking chairs. Elaine was five days past due now, and he was beginning to wonder if everything was all right. If she didn't have this baby pretty soon, he was going to lose what was left of his mind.

It didn't help matters that he couldn't explain his antsy behavior to his co-workers. Elaine still preferred to keep their relationship private. And, looking at the powdered sugar that adorned Ray's nose and chin as he polished off the rest of Debbie's Danish, he couldn't say that he blamed her. He rolled his eyes. These clowns would certainly be no help.

Even his mother's assurance that he'd been two weeks late when she'd gone into labor with him hadn't enabled him sleep any better last night.

Debbie studied him thoughtfully. "You haven't joined us for Friday night at The Pub in ages. Why don't you come with us tonight? Get out and have a little fun." She grinned. "They've got a new karaoke machine. You have to hear Stu sing 'Feelings.' It's really horrible."

"Hey." Stu looked wounded.

As the conversation turned to the Friday night hit parade at The Pub, Brent's thoughts wandered back to Elaine. She was even more anxious than he was. So far everyone from birth class had had their babies without a hitch, but that didn't stop Elaine from worrying about her own imminent labor. And he had to admit that he himself would be much happier once the whole thing was over. Well, maybe not happier, exactly, but at least he and Elaine could get back to their respective lives.

Shifting uncomfortably in his chair, the thought of relinquishing his role in her personal life saddened him. The dismal prospect of a future spent listening to Stu sing "Feelings" every Friday night loomed depressingly ahead.

Unfortunately he'd allowed himself to become a little more attached to Elaine than he'd planned on. He dreaded going back to eating his dinner alone. And he dreaded missing the way her eyes lit up when he came into her bedroom every night, missing the curve of her lips when she smiled at him, the smell of her fragrant hair, the lilt of her throaty laughter as they shared a joke . . . but mostly, he supposed, he dreaded not being needed anymore.

A little more attached than he'd planned. Ha. Talk about denial. He was in this thing way over his head and he knew it.

Balancing his elbows on the break room table, Brent cradled his head in his hands and gingerly massaged his throbbing temples. No, he was beginning to realize, simply working with her here at the station in the future wouldn't be the same at all. She was completely different here at work than she was at home. At home she was free to be herself with him. Here she was the boss, and they would have to go back to their respective roles.

He exhaled mightily, wishing he could blow away the hollow feeling in his gut. The room had grown strangely quiet, and as Brent surfaced from his reverie, he noticed all eyes were trained curiously on the break room door. Turning in his chair, he followed their gaze. Elaine, her cheeks unusually flushed, was leaning unsteadily against the doorjamb. His heart began to thud erratically in his chest.

For crying out loud, she was supposed to be at home in bed. What could be so important that she couldn't wait for him to bring it home tonight? Pushing his chair back from the table, his eyes glittered dangerously at her.

"What the hell are you doing here?"

"Is that any way to address your boss?" she snapped. Shuffling over to the couch behind him, she lowered herself awkwardly into its depth. "Besides, if memory serves, I work here. At least I used to," she muttered, aware of the furtive glances exchanged by her subordinates.

The muscles in Brent's jaw jumped angrily as he stood, nearly knocking his chair over in the process. "You should be in bed."

The collective group of eyes swung from Brent back to Elaine, soaking up with fascination this unusual byplay between their producer and the newest member of the news team.

"My water broke this morning while I was fixing my breakfast. I thought I'd swing by here and pick you up on my way to the hospital." Leaning back on the couch, Elaine swung her feet up onto the cushions and, for once, enjoyed the slack-jawed and bug-eyed reaction of the gossipmongers at the table, as they shifted their eager focus back to Brent.

The blood drained from Brent's face as he sank back down into his chair in shock.

"You...what?" he stammered.

"Her water broke," Stu supplied helpfully.

"Oh. Right." Brent tried to swallow as he struggled to recall what Nurse Shocktaag had instructed, once the bag of waters ruptured. "Okay, okay..." He raked his hands through his hair. "Everyone, stay calm," he ordered, wishing to hell he could follow his own advice.

"Wow," Debbie murmured, looking in admiration at Elaine. "You're doing great. Not like that woman I saw last night on 'Rescue Cops.'"

Ray leaned forward, his eyes animated. "I saw that," he cried exuberantly. "Man, that was something."

"Yeah." Debbie's nod was emphatic as she turned back to Elaine. "This woman's water broke while she was on the Ferris wheel. And she started having these horrible contractions immediately. So she starts screaming, but the guy operating the Ferris wheel was off smoking or something, anyway—"

"Smoking, right!" Ray interrupted, swept up in the story.

"Right, right—" Debbie waved him aside "—anyway the baby was coming. I mean, then and there! Can you believe it? I didn't know they let pregnant women even ride those things...."

"I think it's okay, if it's not the kind of ride that throws you all around," Stu interjected.

Brent's head swam as he watched Elaine smiling benignly at the news crew as they regaled her with the horrors of childbirth. Shouldn't he be timing her contractions? Or boiling water? Or, according to Debbie, preparing to deliver this baby right here in the break room? And why didn't Elaine seem the least bit worried?

Taking a deep breath, he willed himself to get a grip on his runaway pulse. This was no time to panic. No. There was no time for that. Panicking was not good. So he wouldn't. Panic, that is.

Thank heavens they'd canned "The Miracle of Life" idea. Because there was no way in hell he'd ever be able to document his own name, let alone the birth of Elaine's baby.

Standing, he crossed over to Elaine and squeezed between her and her sudden admiration society. "Come on now," he barked, his frayed nerves jangling. "You guys give her some air, will you?" He reached down and pulled her to her feet. "Stay calm and whatever you do, don't panic," he advised, more to himself than anyone.

Elaine felt as though she were standing in the eye of a hurricane. "I'm calm," she assured him, smiling as her usually calm, cool and collected star reporter struggled to shove his head through the sleeve of his jacket. Good heavens, she thought, watching him battle his way into his poor, tangled garment, if they made it through this day, it would be a miracle.

She could hardly believe it. It was finally happening. A shiver of excitement ran down her spine. They were having a baby. Lost in thought, she watched Brent spin in circles, chasing his sleeve, until the first contraction hit.

Panting, she grabbed Brent's arm and forced him to stop for a moment. She leaned against him, her face ashen as the pain gripped her belly.

"Shecky," she whispered, "get the jet. I'm—" grimacing, she clutched his arm ""—outta here.""

Chapter Seven

"Three centimeters?" Elaine caught Brent's shirttail and tugged him over to the hospital bed where she'd been laboring for the past several hours. "That can't be right," she groaned, and pushed the damp strands of hair away from her face with a free hand. "I was dilated to three centimeters an hour ago." Apparently she could forget having this baby anytime soon. Ten centimeters seemed a grueling lifetime away.

"You're making progress, Elaine," Brent reassured her. "You're effacing, and that's what's important here. Remember?"

"Umm." She smiled weakly up at him, then tried to focus her attention on the formidable Nurse Shocktaag as she bustled in and out of the room. The efficient woman was preparing the equipment Dr. Hanson would require when the time came. And it couldn't come soon enough to suit her, Elaine thought, wincing as she grasped Brent's bicep in a death grip. The pain was unbearable. Couldn't the old biddy see that? What was taking so blasted long? She wanted drugs, and she wanted them now.

"I demand a recount," she whimpered up at Brent as he leaned over her and lightly stroked her cheek with the backs of his fingers.

The birthing suite at Chicago Central was cheerfully decorated in lovely shades of pastel, with a window seat that made into a bed for the labor coach, a television and stereo for the patient's entertainment pleasure and a tasteful seating area for guests. Elaine would most likely have found herself enjoying her stay if it weren't for the excruciating cramps that seized her midsection every two minutes.

Brent reached over to the small table situated next to the hospital bed, retrieved a cool, damp cloth and arranged it over Elaine's forehead.

"Hang in there, honey," he encouraged. "Ruby says that the anesthesiologist should be here in about an hour or so. Once you get the epidural you'll feel a lot better."

Elaine shot him a withering look. "Oh, sure. Easy for you to say. I can't wait that long," she gasped and then moaned. "At this point I'd settle for a quick blow to the head with a hammer."

Chuckling sympathetically, Brent lifted the cloth from her forehead and replaced it with his lips, bestowing a tender kiss. "There," he murmured, "does that help?"

"Umm," Elaine nodded and sighed. "Some."

He really was very sweet. Why hadn't she ever noticed what a rock he was before? How could she have mistaken his quiet strength for the country bumpkin she'd pigeonholed him to be when he'd joined the WCH news team last year? Just never took the time to look beneath the outdated clothes and ugly horn-rims, she guessed. At any rate she was incredibly grateful for his steady, fortifying presence.

"Thanks," she whispered as he dropped an ice chip into her mouth. She'd never been so thirsty in her life.

Leaning back against the cool, crisp linen case that covered her pillow, she wondered why anyone in her right mind would ever have more than one baby. Why, some people actually went through labor a half a dozen times or more. Good heavens, were they masochists? At this point she couldn't imagine ever wanting to have another child.

She inhaled deeply and glanced over at Brent. Thank God he was here for her. He was the only thing that kept her going. Her salvation, really. Elaine had to admit, as she watched him thoughtfully studying the baby monitor that was attached to her abdomen, he was right about how much she would need him.

It was amazing how comfortable she was, having him here. He was the only person she could envision sharing this moment with. The only person she felt sure would understand her vast array of emotions. Both the pain and the joy. Because between contractions, she could almost relax long enough to become excited about meeting Sara and Bobby's baby.

Whoosh, whoosh, whoosh. The sweet life song penetrated her reverie.

She closed her eyes and listened to the reassuring sound of the baby's strong heartbeat coming from the machine that Brent hovered so protectively over, when he wasn't busy being her bastion of strength. The steady rhythm reminded her that it was all worth it. Every last pain. Ruby had explained earlier that the monitor that churned out endless yards of white graph paper kept track of both the fetal heartbeat and her contractions. Fascinated by the buttons and dials, Brent had taken to the machine like a cowboy to his horse. She smiled as he pushed his glasses up higher on the bridge of his nose.

"Clark," she whispered, catching his attention. "I don't suppose you could talk that old killjoy, Shocktaag into some pain medication before the anesthesiologist gets here?"

Turning his attention from the hypnotic thrumming of the baby's heartbeat, Brent removed his glasses and smiled sympathetically. "I'll ask her just as soon as she comes back," he assured her.

Elaine regarded him through her half-closed eyelids. "That would be great."

It was odd how she'd never really noticed how nice looking he was before, either. Without those glasses, he was really quite handsome, she mused, trying to busy her mind with something other than the impending contraction that lurked just ahead. He even managed to look quite fetching in that faded gray sweatshirt and those impossibly tight jeans he'd retrieved from the trunk of his car once they'd arrived at the hospital. Come to think of it, that outfit suited him. In the future, she would also spend more time appreciating the advantages of casual wear, she thought, eyeing his narrow hips and well-muscled thighs.

But not now. No. Now she was going to have a contraction.

Noticing the look of pain that flashed across her face, Brent glanced at the monitor and nodded. "It looks like you're going into another contraction," he told her and took her hand. "Come on now, sweetheart, breathe." His eyes locked with hers as he began the breathing pattern they'd learned in class.

He whispered encouragement, and she nodded, transfixed on his face. Cast adrift on a sea of pain, Elaine clung to the lifeline that was Brent's strong hand. Focusing on his unwavering gaze, she weathered yet another contraction and allowed her mind to take flight. And it was then, as a barrage of muddled, incoherent thoughts flitted through her subconscious, that she began to realize just how much she'd come to depend on Brent.

There was no way she'd ever have been able to go through this by herself, she knew, as he led her to the crest of the pain and down the other side. He was not only her partner and coach, he was her friend. Somehow he'd managed to sneak past her arsenal of defensive weapons and worm his way into her heart. Great. Just what she needed. To fall in love with a co-worker.

Fall in love? That couldn't be right. She was probably just confused from the pain. Or was she? If being in love meant needing and wanting someone as badly as she'd come to need and want to be near him, then she had it for him, and she had it bad.

"Ohhh," she moaned, wrestling with a pain in her heart that had absolutely no connection to bearing this child. This couldn't be happening. She was setting herself up for a terrible fall. What man in reasonable control of his faculties would want someone as unlovable as herself? And then again, there was the matter of the ready-made family she was preparing to bring into this world.... *"Ohhh."* She writhed and moaned again.

"I'm so sorry, honey. I know it hurts. Hang on, though. Ruby just came back, and I'll see about getting you something for the pain."

His gentle expression was so sympathetic, Elaine wanted to weep. How would she ever be able to get through another day without him? He left her side, and she watched while Brent briefly conferred with Nurse Shocktaag. A moment later he returned, smiling triumphantly, Ruby at his side.

"So, you are ready for some relief?" The older woman peered down her pointed nose at Elaine and nodded curtly.

"Yes," Elaine breathed, wishing there were an immunization for broken hearts in the competent nurse's bag of tricks.

Brent laced his fingers with hers as Ruby administered a dose of pain medication into the IV. The drug began to take effect almost immediately.

"Is that a little better?" he asked, squinting at the printout of the baby's heartbeat as it rolled out of the monitor.

Feeling suddenly intoxicated, Elaine smiled giddily. "Yessssir," she slurred and pulled his hand up to her cheek. "Lotss better. Hey," her head lolled onto his hand as she gazed up at him. "Thankss. You're so nice. I know," she continued, feeling suddenly quite glib, "that I haven't told you how much all your help meanss to me. But, it doess. Really." She could feel her eyes drifting shut, and she continued woozily, "I love it. You. I mean...I...love...you....."

Nurse Shocktaag smiled at Brent as the anesthesiologist arrived in the room along with a younger nurse. "Allow her to rest for a moment. And you take a break. I will stay with her while she gets the epidural. I will come for you when we are done." She pointed at the door and shooed him toward it. "Go. Go. Eat some lunch."

Dazed, Brent nodded and, following her instructions, moved across the room, through the blurry haze of Elaine's announcement and into the hallway. His stomach crowded into his throat as he wandered down the hall through the OB wing and stopped before a large plate glass window. He felt his eyes glaze over as he stared out the window and over the endless expanse of Lake Michigan. Oblivious to the colorful sailboats that skimmed bravely over the water's choppy surface beneath the cloudy fall sky, he tried to assimilate the meaning of Elaine's words.

She had said she loved him! Never mind that she was under the influence of heaven only knew what. On some level he was sure that the truth had surfaced.

Then again, there were many different kinds of love, and he doubted that Elaine could ever feel for him as deeply as he'd come to feel for her. The fragile bubble of excitement burst as reality dawned. It was just the drug talking. He'd do well to keep that in mind. Feeling as though the wind in his own sail had abruptly died, he turned away from the window and slogged down to the hospital cafeteria in search of something edible.

If ever he needed his strength, it was now.

She looked like an angel. Too bad the gang at the station couldn't see their Barracuda now. Brent stood next to Elaine's bed and watched her sleep. The epidural had evidently worked its magic, and she was sound asleep, exhausted after a morning of some pretty heavy suffering. Her face, so girlish in repose, drew him like a magnet, and he was unable to resist touching his lips to the smooth porcelain of her cheeks. He'd never be able to understand how, even in the throes of labor, and without a speck of makeup, she managed to look so beautiful.

Full lips, almond-shaped eyes fringed with thick, dark lashes, high cheekbones ... If this baby managed to inherit even one of these attributes from her side of the family, it would be an amazingly handsome child.

If he could, he would gladly suffer the pain in her place. He hated the feeling of helplessness that overcame him as she endured each increasingly painful contraction. Picking up one of her delicate hands in his, he rubbed it absently with the pad of his thumb. Now, more than ever before, he admired her strength. Elaine Lewis was an amazing woman.

She stirred in her sleep, and he backed away from the bed and settled onto the window seat where he could keep an eye on her. He was tired, but knew that he was far too keyed up to drift off. Soon the baby would make its appearance, and he didn't want to miss a second of the impending miracle.

No, he would just put his feet up and rest for a moment. He'd stay awake. Elaine might ... need ... him....

Elaine was groggy. Her eyelids felt as though they weighed a ton, and her mouth was so parched she was sure that if she didn't drink at least a gallon of water within the next minute or two, she'd die of thirst. Rolling her head to a more comfortable position on the pillow, Ruby's tight, gray bun came into view as the older woman bent over the fetal monitor.

She touched her tongue to her dry lips in an effort to moisten them, but it was almost as if someone had packed her mouth with cotton. "Where is Brent?" she whispered hoarsely, tapping the bed rail to gain the nurse's attention.

"Shh," Ruby rightened to her usual ramrod posture and touched a bony finger to her tightly pursed lips. "He sleeps by the window. He is very tired from helping all day. I tell

him to take more breaks, but he is protective, no?" A be-
grudging smile tipped the corners of her mouth.

Elaine shifted her gaze to the window seat, where she
found Brent sprawled out, one arm flung over his eyes, the
other, dangling off the edge of his bed. Her heart constricted at the touching sight, and she felt her eyes grow
misty. The shadows of his lashes rested lightly across his
cheeks, and his strongly chiseled lips puffed softly as his
chest rose and fell with the breath of deep slumber.

"You know," Ruby whispered in a rare moment of
chummy candor, "I never see a father so excited as this one.
He is a lovely man."

"Yes." Elaine's gaze swung back to the prunish woman.
"Yes, he is."

As the shifts changed, Ruby efficiently introduced the
nurses who would be assisting in the birth once she left, then
she squeezed Elaine's knee with her knobby hand. "You will
be fine with these girls," she told her, indicating the cheery-
faced Sandy and Clarejoy. "I wish you both luck," she said,
her hawklike eyes darting from her to Brent as he slept. "I
have a feeling you will be just right as parents, no? Love
each other and love the little one."

Suddenly Elaine desperately wanted the curmudgeonly
woman to stay. She felt the childish urge to burst into tears
and beg her to work yet another shift. But even the militant
nurse must have a family that she had to get home to, Elaine
knew. Everyone had families, it seemed. Everyone but herself. Family had never been important to her before. But
now, as she watched Ruby fuss with her covers, she desperately longed for her mother's soothing presence and a husband to call her own. Someone to walk out of the hospital
with her and into the rest of her life. Resisting the tears that
threatened at Ruby's imminent departure, she set her chin
bravely.

"Thank you," she murmured. "I'll see you at the birth
class reunion."

"Ahh, yes." Ruby's sudden smile was radiant. "You will meet the babies. That Olsen baby...he is a cutie. Life has some pleasant surprises, no?" On that note she turned without a backward glance and marched out the door.

Feeling bereft, Elaine smiled tentatively as the nurse Ruby had introduced as Sandy snapped on a pair of latex gloves.

"Hi, there," Sandy said, smiling, and looked down into Elaine's face. "I'm going to be taking care of you during transition, and once the baby is here, I'll assist Dr. Hanson, while Clarejoy takes care of your newborn. But first, I want to see how far we've come."

"Okay," Elaine sighed and submitted to yet another check to discover how far she'd managed to dilate while she slept.

Sandy finished her task and nodded approvingly at Elaine. "Good job." She pulled off her gloves. "I'll call Dr. Hanson now. And we'll get the anesthesiologist back here to turn down your epidural so you'll be able to feel the contractions. You, my dear, are ready to start pushing."

"I am?" Elaine's eyes grew wide with wonder. Dilating from zero to three had been much worse than three to ten. Thank heavens for modern science.

"Yes indeedy," she chirped, motioning for Clarejoy to give her a hand preparing Elaine's bed for birth.

The bed came apart in the middle and the lower section was whisked away, and two footrests were attached in its place. Equipment was rearranged around the bed, and Sandy briefed Elaine on the use of the handlebars at the side of the bed.

"Just hold these like so," she instructed, "and when the time comes, use them to help yourself bear down." Pressing a button at the side of the bed, she elevated the back to an angle more conducive to childbirth.

"And," Elaine quipped, "if it gets too rough, I can just peddle on out of here, right?"

Sandy laughed. "You might want to wait until after the baby comes. And judging from the look of things, that will be pretty soon now."

Elaine felt a pleasant flush steal into her cheeks. Sara's baby was coming. Ruby was right, she decided, glancing over at the still-deeply sleeping Brent. Life did have a few pleasant surprises.

Brent had no idea how long he'd been asleep, when the sound of Dr. Hanson's voice roused him. Jumping to a standing position, he stumbled to Elaine's side on wobbly legs, rubbing his eyes and feeling guilty at having fallen asleep. The room had mysteriously transformed from the comfy suite at the Ritz, to a sterile labor room. Ruby had disappeared and been replaced by two younger nurses, and Elaine was chatting calmly with Dr. Hanson.

He felt strangely left out of the proceedings. They all seemed to be getting along just fine without him. Fighting the temptation to feel sorry for himself, he tucked his shirt-tails into his jeans, straightened the sweatshirt he wore over that, and waited patiently for someone to notice him. Much to his relief, it was worth the wait.

The smile Elaine bestowed upon him could have thawed an iceberg with its warmth.

"It's about time you woke up, sleepyhead," she teased, sounding drained. Her smile faded. "I'm glad you're here." She clasped his hand in a firm grip and winced. "They turned off my epidural. I'm starting to feel the pain again." She moaned.

"This is it, then," Brent said and glanced at the monitor. She was having a contraction, and it looked like a big one if the squiggly lines on the graph paper were any indication. Squeezing her hand to get her attention, he lowered his face to hers and began coaching, as Dr. Hanson adjusted his stool and studied his tray of tools down at the other end of the bed.

"Yesss." The word came out as a painful hiss from between Elaine's lips. "This is it," she said, panting.

Seconds ticked past, turning into minutes, which in turn became an hour. Contractions came and went, gaining in momentum and intensity, until Brent was sure Elaine would never make it to the end. Actually, he was almost more worried about making it to the end himself. He didn't want to alarm Elaine with his worries, but as the sands sifted through the hourglass, he was beginning to wonder if this baby would ever be born. Did it always take this long? he wondered. He had a sudden new and profound respect for his mother.

Dr. Hanson seemed to feel that everything was progressing nicely, so Brent decided he would just have to take his word for it. Still, if he felt this drained, he could only begin to imagine what Elaine must be going through.

Elaine moaned audibly with each breath. "Ohhh..."

"Shh, honey. Save your energy. Try to breathe slower." Brent pushed several damp strands of hair out of her eyes as she writhed in pain. He reached for the cup of ice and held a chip to her lips.

"*You* breathe slower," she ordered, her eyes wild. "Get that away from me." She pushed at the cup in his hand. "I...think...I'm...hyper...ventilating," she managed to whisper, her shadowed eyes were filled with fear. "Brent...I can't...stop.... Ohhh..."

"Elaine. Listen to me." He grasped her face between his hands and looked into her eyes. "Breathe with me. Elaine. Breathe with me, honey." He fell into one of the patterns they'd learned in class, breathing slowly, his eyes locked with hers, and as though hypnotized, Elaine followed his lead. "That's better. Good girl," he praised.

"Where is the ice?"

"Here." He picked up the cup she'd pushed away earlier and ran a cube over her lips.

"Thanks," she whispered gratefully, and gazed up at him, adoration filling her eyes. "Sorry I'm such a grouch. I think I've been invaded by aliens."

"Hey. You're doing just great. I'm proud of you."

"You are?" She looked up at him for his approval, her girlish vulnerability obliterating any trace of Elaine Lewis, corporate broadcaster.

Here their roles had reversed. Here he was in command, and she was subject to his leadership. He had to admit it was refreshing for a change. "Yes. I am."

"Oh, Brent," she clutched his hand in what felt to him like an attempt to amputate his thumb with her fingernails. Lifting her head off the pillow, she hunched forward. "Here we go again." She cried out in agony as she assisted Sara's little life into the world.

This next contraction finally brought the baby's head to a bulging crown.

"Good job," Dr. Hanson said. "Just a couple more pushes and I can introduce you to your baby."

Electric jolts of excitement shot down Brent's spine. He felt like a kid at Christmas. Only this was a million times better. This was quite possibly the most exciting, most beautiful thing he'd ever experienced.

"I feel another one," Elaine moaned, weak with exhaustion. "But I'm too tired to push anymore." She suddenly burst into tears and looked up at Brent with panic-stricken eyes. "I can't do this, Brent. Really. I want to stop. Let's just call it a day, okay? Please. Tell them I want to go home now," she pleaded, growing increasingly hysterical with fright. "Brent . . . oh, Brent. It hurts so bad."

He let go of his heart forever in that moment, as it went out to her in her pain. It amazed him how a heart so swollen with love for another human being could continue to beat. Once again Brent pulled her eyes into his steady, unwavering gaze. "Elaine. Listen to me now, honey. The baby is almost here. If you can summon enough energy for just one or two more pushes, the pain will stop and it will all be over. Then," he promised, coaxing her to relax, "we can go home. Okay?"

"Okay." She managed to grit this out through her tightly clenched jaw.

The raw trust in her expression was unmistakable. It was heady stuff, and Brent vowed then and there that he would always—if she would allow it—be there for her in some capacity or another.

"Brent."

"I know." He could see that she had to bear down. Her lithe body quaked with her effort, and beads of sweat broke out anew on her forehead. His eyes penetrated hers, and together they rode the crest of the pain.

"Terrific!" Dr. Hanson pulled his rolling tray of tools closer to his side. "Once more, Elaine."

"Is it born yet?" she asked, delirious from the tidal waves of torment that washed over her.

"The head!" Brent crowed, jubilantly, leaving her side briefly to inspect the baby. "The head is here! And, Elaine, it looks great. Beautiful. Awesome."

Time seemed to suspend for Brent, as Elaine, with one final grunt, expelled the tiny life from the safe haven of her body. The baby emerged, red-faced and squalling, its arms waving jerkily in the sudden freedom of the surrounding space. A giant lump thickly crowded Brent's throat as he moved toward Dr. Hanson to get a better look at the newborn.

It was a girl. A healthy, gorgeous baby girl.

"Elaine. We have a girl," he managed to say, past the growing emotional obstruction in his air passage. And, for the first time since he was a small boy living in his mother's home back in Iowa, he felt tears spring unbidden to his eyes. "She's beautiful, Elaine."

Sandy peered indulgently at the baby and then up at Brent. "She sure looks like her daddy."

Knowing that this was impossible, Brent, nevertheless, felt his chest swell with pride.

"Thanks." He beamed at the nurse.

Elaine's smile was tremulous.

He moved back to her side and smoothed her hair away from her face, feeling the dampness from the tears that flowed down her cheeks. Perching next to her on the bed, he gathered her into his embrace, their tears of awe and happiness mingling as he kissed her and held her tight.

Elaine relaxed against the strong wall of Brent's chest as Dr. Hanson placed the baby on her tummy for a moment while he clamped and severed the umbilical cord. The baby's tiny, mewling cry reminded her of the bleat of a spring lamb, and she looked up at Brent, her eyes glistening.

"She is beautiful, isn't she?"

"Like her mother."

Elaine leaned forward and touched her lips to the incredibly soft skin of the baby's cheek. And as the tiny eyes blinked up at her, seeming to contain the wisdom of the ages, she again heard the echo of Sara's sweet voice.

Love her, Elaine, it seemed to say. *Love her.*

Chapter Eight

"You know, we're going to have to think of something to call her other than 'Peanut.'"

Brent smiled over at Elaine from the rocking chair he occupied next to her bed in the birthing suite. Looking fondly down into the sleeping face of the cherub he held in his arms, he said, "It kind of suits her now, but I can't imagine her going through life with that handle."

Elaine laughed. Nearly twenty-four hours had passed since the baby had been born, and after some sporadic sleep during the night, she was beginning to feel a little bit like her old self. Long shadows from the setting sun slanted in through the window, and a single lamp in the corner of the room glowed cheerily. They would spend one more night in the hospital before they were discharged in the morning.

"You're right." She sighed, turning onto her side so that she could watch Brent rock the tiny bundle in his arms. "Peanut Lewis, CEO, just doesn't make it."

"Neither does Grandma Peanut. Not very adult." He laughed as the baby yawned and stretched in her sleep. The beginnings of a light beard shadowed his square jaw, and once again Elaine found herself marveling at how she'd never noticed his good looks before. Clearly she spent far too much time glued to a video monitor. Her eyes wandered to his well-shaped hands as he stroked the soft fuzz that adorned the top of the baby's head.

"She sure does sleep a lot," he commented. Leaning back he rolled the baby onto her stomach across his chest.

Already he handled the baby like a pro. Unlike herself. "Hmm. Not really. She woke up at least three times last night, looking for food." Elaine sighed ruefully.

Brent lifted his chin off his chest and looked over at her. "I must have slept through it. How'd it go?"

She felt herself grow warm beneath his unfathomable gaze. "Painful. They never mentioned that particular tidbit in breast-feeding class. I had a whole slew of different nurses in here last night, trying to explain the mechanics. I'm not kidding, Brent, it may look easy, but I swear, you need at least six arms."

His eyes twinkled as he watched her over the top of the baby's head. "Aren't you glad we took that class?"

"I guess. We muddled through while you were in the cafeteria for breakfast and lunch today, but it was mostly a fiasco. They say practice makes perfect, but I'm beginning to wonder." Elaine sent Brent a doubtful look. "I wish we could just give her a sandwich."

Brent chuckled and peered down at the baby. "Would you like a sandwich?" He pretended to listen as she nuzzled his neck. "Nope. She says she'll wait till she has some teeth."

Smiling, Elaine pulled the blanket up over her shoulders and gazed on in contentment as Brent closed his eyes and slowly rocked the baby.

It had been a wonderful day. The station had sent a giant bouquet of flowers along with a card expressing best wishes, and some of the news crew had stopped by with gifts for the baby. She smiled at the image of Stu and Ray awkwardly holding the infant, blushing delightedly when she'd gripped their fingers with her tiny hands. Debbie had accompanied them, complaining loudly that they were hogging the baby. Not to mention the fact that the silly men were holding her all wrong. The young woman had rolled her eyes in feminine camaraderie at Elaine, and for the first time, Elaine had begun to feel like one of the gang.

Although, she had a sneaking suspicion that they were more interested in her relationship with Brent than they were in the baby... but it was nice to have visitors. She'd been beginning to wonder if anyone would remember her at all. But even Brent's mother had wired a lovely plant. She'd have to send her a thank-you card, she thought making a mental note. Margaret Clark must be a wonderful woman— her eyes strayed from the leafy foliage back to Brent—because she certainly had a wonderful son.

And then there were the roses. Their delicate scent filled the room. One dozen of the most beautiful red roses she'd ever laid eyes on. From Brent. She couldn't remember the last time anyone had given her roses, and his thoughtful gesture meant more to her than she could ever say.

"So," Brent murmured, his eyes still closed, "what'll it be?"

"What?"

"Her name?"

"Oh." Elaine's brow puckered as a wave of melancholy washed over her. "I don't know. What do you think about Sara?" It seemed only fitting, she mused, wishing she knew what her cousin and her husband had planned to name their child.

Brent opened his eyes and slowly smiled at her. "I love it."

"Me, too."

They smiled indulgently at the baby for a moment before he asked, "What about her middle name?"

Elaine's eyes found his. "I'd love to name her after you." She frowned. "But Sara Brent is a little strange. Why don't you pick?"

He beamed. "I've always been partial to Margaret. For my mother."

"Margaret." Elaine rolled the word across her tongue, as though sampling an expensive wine. "We could call her Meg."

"How about that, Meg?" Brent looked proudly down at the baby, who chose that moment to open her eyes. "She likes it," he decided. "You know," he confided uneasily, glancing up at Elaine, "the nurse brought in a packet of paperwork for us to fill out this morning."

"Oh?"

He nodded and continued to gently rock the baby. "Now that we've chosen her name, I can fill out the birth announcement for the newspaper. But that still leaves the question of the birth certificate."

Elaine was puzzled. "What's the problem?"

The rocker squeaked pleasantly as his eyes darted from the baby to her and back to the baby again. "I need to know who to write down as mother."

Her brow furrowed. That was a good question. Sara was, after all, the biological mother. But she was the birth mother. The baby squirmed and clutched a handful of Brent's shirt in her tiny fist, and Elaine's heart constricted painfully. By all rights, it should be Bobby and Sara rocking their newborn. It should be Bobby and Sara filling out the paperwork, receiving congratulations, celebrating life.

Life. Sometimes it was so unbelievably fragile. As she contemplated the little orphan who rested—unaware of the tragic circumstances of her birth—in Brent's strong arms, she made a decision. A decision of which she felt sure both Sara and Bobby would approve. Maybe she was just caught up in the post-partum emotional aftermath. Or maybe it was raging hormones. She would probably never know for sure. But, if she had any choice in the matter, this child would have a live mother and father to call her own.

"Put me down for the mother." Her eyes caught his and held. "And," she suggested shyly, "put yourself down for the father." Elaine braced herself for his refusal. She wouldn't blame him for declining the nomination. That would certainly go far above and beyond the call of duty as a caring labor coach. Still, even though it meant setting herself up for possible humiliation, she wanted to give him the chance. He was the closest thing to a father little Meg would probably ever have.

Brent stopped rocking, his eyes wide. "Me?"

"No, no," she hastily reassured him, backpedaling some. "Not if you don't want to, of course. I doubt that it would be legally binding or anything, and you wouldn't be obligated to care for her in the future, I was just thinking that, you know, since you were here for the birth and, you know—" she continued, babbling, embarrassed "—she doesn't have any family at all, no one to teach her how to play ball, or whatever it is that a father does...."

"Elaine—" Brent interrupted in exasperation "—shut up."

Mortified, her eyes flew to her hands as she nervously plucked the balls of fluff from her blanket. He was right. It was a foolish idea. She didn't know what had possessed her.

"I would be honored." His voice was hushed, filled with emotion and his eyes were suddenly bright.

"You would?" she whispered, afraid that if she spoke out loud, she could break the magic spell that seemed to bind the three of them together.

He pressed his lips to Meg's downy curls. "I wouldn't have it any other way," he whispered back, grinning foolishly.

Elaine hobbled painfully across the room and eyed her suitcase. It was checkout time. Time to leave the relative safety of the hospital and rejoin the real world. Time to begin her new life as mother to little Sara Margaret. The prospect seemed overwhelming, considering she needed help just getting in and out of bed. How would she ever manage?

"We're all squared away at the front desk," Brent informed her, coming briskly back into the room. "So, if you're ready, I'll take you home."

"I guess so," she responded warily. "I still have some packing to do...."

"It's okay. Take your time. We still have several hours before we have to be out of here." His eyes searched the suite. "What did you do with the car seat?"

Elaine stopped in her tracks and slowly turned to face him. "What car seat?"

Dragging his fingers through his hair, Brent sighed. "We don't have a car seat?"

"Uh...no. I didn't know we'd need one."

He nodded. "It's the law. What about some clothes and diapers and things for the baby? The stuff she's wearing now belongs to the hospital. Except for the disposable diaper she's got on," he amended.

She shrugged and gripped the handrails of the bed for support. Man. She felt as though she'd been run over by a truck. Everything ached. Even her hair. "I didn't think about that," she breathed, wanting desperately to sit down, but fearing the consequences.

Brent snorted. "Well, we can't exactly take her home naked, now can we? It's cold out there."

Tears threatened the already tenuous hold she had on her composure. She was a terrible mother. So far she was miserable at feeding the innocent creature that was her daughter and a complete failure at clothing her. Not to mention the fact that she had no way to get the poor kid home. This was much harder than she'd expected.

Seeming to read her considerable distress, Brent strode to her side and helped her over to the window seat. "Oh, honey, don't cry. I'm sorry. I know you didn't have much chance to get out and shop. I should have thought of that."

"It's just that...huh," she blubbered, "Dr. Hanson told me I couldn't ... huh g-g-get out of bed...."

He sank down beside her and pulled her into his arms. "Shh. Hey. Why don't I go get us a car seat and a few clothes and meet you back here in a couple hours. You pack and get the baby fed." He peered into her face, then kissed her eyelids.

She nestled into his comforting embrace, never wanting to leave the security she found there. He smelled pleasantly of a masculine mixture of spicy soap and after-shave, and his heartbeat thudded reassuringly beneath her cheek. Locking her arms around his trim waist, she exhaled contentedly and asked, "How will you know what to get?"

His lips twitched in amusement. "I'll ask. That's my job, remember? Asking questions?"

Pushing her hair away from her face, she smiled, feeling suddenly buoyant. "Thanks." Everything would be all right. Brent was there.

He brushed his lips quickly across hers before he stood. "Get dressed. I'll take care of everything."

Yes, she thought, watching him leave the room, *he would.*

Brent pulled the station's remote van to a stop in front of Elaine's house and hopped out. Coming around to the passenger side, he opened the door and helped her untangle the car seat from the safety belt that held the peacefully sleeping Meg securely in place.

"Really, Brent," she said with a resigned sigh. "I don't know why you had to abscond with the company van. Are you trying to get us both fired?"

Grinning, he assisted her to her feet and lifted the car seat into his arms. "Stop bossing me around," he commanded her good-naturedly. "We're not at work."

Elaine shook her head. "You're getting a little too big for your britches, buddy," she teased, and taking his arm, walked with him to her front door. Feeling suddenly awkward, she searched for the words to thank him for everything he'd done as he opened her front door and let them inside. It was then that reality dawned. He was leaving. How was she going to do this without her partner? Her heart thudded dismally.

She looked around at the familiar walls, trying to orient herself and quell the panic she felt rising at the prospect of single motherhood. Strange, how her home looked exactly the same, when everything else in her life had turned on its ear she mused, slinging her purse onto her coffee table and turning to make her goodbyes.

"Brent," she began, and then discovered she was talking to herself. Meg blinked up at her from where Brent had planted her on the sofa, her miniature toes peeking out from beneath her new blanket. "You is not Brent," she said in affectionate, motherly gibberish. "You is Meg." Her heart swelled with love as the baby sneezed, then looked at her with owlish surprise.

Where had he disappeared to? she wondered. Moving to the window, she watched in mute amazement as he opened the back of the van and began unloading what appeared to be a mountain of baby paraphernalia. Realizing her mouth was hanging open, she snapped it shut and smiled. From the look of things, he'd purchased the entire infant section from some lucky store.

"Where do you want this stuff?" He grunted, wrestling a huge box that obviously contained a crib through her front door.

"Uh," she said, limping over to the hallway that led to the spare bedroom and pointing at the door. "In there, I guess. What on earth have you done?"

"Don't give me a hard time about this, Elaine," he insisted, depositing the crib in the room. "You're going to need this stuff, and I didn't have time to consult you about decor and the like." Brushing past her, he headed out to the van for another load. And another. And... another....

Brent nearly wore a path in her snow-white carpet as he delivered his booty. A changing table, several boxes of disposable diapers, a battery-operated swing, a deluxe stroller, a bassinet, an infant bathing tub—complete with rubber ducky, a half dozen bags of odds and ends for baby maintenance and enough clothing to see Meg well into the first grade.

"I don't suppose you have a partridge in a pear tree in there?" Elaine murmured, sure now more than ever that she was head over heels in love with this crazy cowboy.

Staggering under the weight of a highchair and a host of stuffed animals, Brent shook his head. "No... the lady at Baby World didn't mention that," he responded, taking her seriously. "But I've got several bears, bunnies and a lamb that bleats somewhere in here." He dumped his load in the middle of her living room.

"Hey, Lainey," he enthused, unconsciously calling her by Sara's nickname for her, "take a look at this." Rummaging around in the pile, he found and withdrew a Mother Goose mobile and wound it up. The tune to "Rock-a-bye Baby" tinkled as the little chicks slowly rotated. "When the bough breaks," he sang softly along, "the cradle will fall, and down will come baby—" he looked over at Meg, his eyes loving "—cradle and all."

How had she gotten so lucky? she wondered, sending a silent prayer of thanksgiving heavenward. She didn't deserve him. She would certainly never be able to thank him.

"Brent," she began helplessly, "I..."

"Hold that thought," he ordered, and rushed back out to the van. Returning moments later with a suitcase and sleeping bag, he closed and locked her front door.

She glanced at him in confusion. "What's that?"

Shrugging, he tossed his bag into a chair and arched his back, stretching his shirt tightly over his fascinating physique. "I stopped by my place and picked up a few things."

"You did?" What was he talking about?

"Yes. You're going to need a hand with the baby. And because you don't have a mother, and knowing that you probably hadn't arranged for a nurse, since you weren't even aware you needed a car seat—" he grinned "—I figured I'd volunteer for the job. That is," he said, pausing uncertainly, "if you'll have me...."

The weakness in her knees was not related to the fact that she had just had a baby. Knowing it was probably a horrendous mistake to grow any more dependent on him than she already was, she heard herself whisper, "I'll have you."

She must be nuts. Everyone she'd ever loved had eventually, one way or another, left her. Would he? It was too depressing to contemplate.

"Great," he breathed, relief spreading over his handsome features. "Great!" Crowing happily, he swept her into his arms and crushed her enthusiastically to his chest until she begged for mercy. They stood, holding each other for a supercharged moment, awareness crackling between them, before Brent lowered his head and touched his lips to hers for a brief moment.

Then, sighing, he squeezed her arms and fought for self-control. She looked far better than any new mother had a right to look, he thought, as she gazed up at him. Battling the urge to kiss her senseless, he released her and forced his eyes to the pile of Meg's new furnishings.

"I guess I'd better get started putting some of this stuff together," he said ruefully. He'd have to keep himself busy. Living with Elaine would definitely test his willpower. Feeling a restless arousal grip his belly, he exhaled deeply and rotated his head from side to side. Perhaps he should have bought the kid a car. One that needed a complete engine overhaul. That would keep him occupied. Because if Elaine kept smiling at him in that unguarded, sexy way, he was going to lose it.

"Elaine, what's wrong?"

"Nothing. Go away," she snapped testily, her frustration obvious even through the nursery door. It sounded to him as though she'd been crying. He took a deep breath. Dealing with this newer, more emotional version of his usually self-confident boss would take some adjustment. And understanding.

"Don't be ridiculous," he cajoled, cracking the door open and poking his head inside. There he found Elaine, sitting in a rocker, staring in dismay at the squalling Meg. He could tell by her fussy cry that the kid was hungry. Why wasn't Elaine feeding her? "What's the problem, Elaine?" he asked, coming over and kneeling down next to her.

She turned her large eyes balefully to him and, hesitating, seemed to search for the words to explain her predicament. She looked almost embarrassed. "Brent, do you remember in class when they taught us how the baby is supposed to latch on to the breast?"

Nodding thoughtfully he responded, "Yes."

A small flicker of hope flared in her eyes. "Oh, good." Her sigh contained quiet desperation. "And do you remember what they said to do if the mother becomes engorged?" She raised her voice to be heard over the baby.

He frowned. "Sort of."

"Sort of? Brent, that's not good enough," she cried. "Think! You have to remember. If you don't I'm afraid this kid is going to starve to death."

Meg's pitiful cry was growing steadily angrier, and Elaine's panic seemed to run parallel to the baby's outrage.

His eyes dropped to her considerable bustline, which was prominent beneath her nightgown, and he immediately averted his eyes. Though breast-feeding was the most natural thing in the world, and it had even been his idea in the first place, there was something incredibly intimate about discussing Elaine's breasts with her. In class it had seemed so clinical. Here it seemed so... personal. "She's not latching on?"

"Obviously not," she complained, bouncing the baby stiffly on her knee. "I don't know how she could, seeing that I have two bowling balls on my chest at the moment. There is nothing to latch on to! Arnold Schwarzenegger couldn't latch on to these babies. I could star in a Madonna video.

Without the metal bra," she nearly shouted, her hysteria rising.

He bit the inside of his cheek to keep from laughing. It was true. She could. As far as he was concerned, she looked great. But telling her that now probably wouldn't win him any points in the tact department.

"Look," he said, rising to his feet and lifting the baby to his arms. "I seem to remember them saying something about wet heat for this kind of problem. Why don't you go take a hot shower and relax? I'll take care of Meg. She won't starve to death, trust me. She's as healthy as a horse."

Elaine looked doubtful.

"Go on. We'll be fine, won't we, sweetheart?" He looked down at Meg who'd grown quiet in his arms.

"Oh, sure," Elaine huffed, as she took his advice and headed slowly toward the door. "She's quiet for you. I think the men should have to feed the baby," she continued grumpily and her voice grew dimmer as she headed—griping all the way—down the hall to the bathroom.

Brent smiled down at the baby. "Be patient, sweetie. She's learning."

A half hour later, Elaine returned, considerably refreshed and ready to try again. Settling herself back into the rocker, she looked up at Brent and held her arms out for the baby. "Umm," she began, feeling quite awkward, "I don't suppose you could give me a hand here. After all, you were pretty good at this in class, as I recall."

"Uh, sure." Brent couldn't quite seem to meet her eyes as he lowered the baby to her lap. "I would try the football hold."

"Right," she said with a grin. "Like I know how to hold a football. Men."

Grinning, but still not able to look at her, Brent positioned the baby in her lap. "Here," he said, his breath tickling her neck as he placed her arms around Meg's tiny body. "Just tuck her feet under your arm and her head should go right about, uh... here." His eyes shot to hers and then to

the wall behind her head as he held the baby to her breast.
"I think you'll be just fine now, so I'll leave you to it," he
said nervously. Slipping his hand from under the baby's
head, it brushed against her breast and even though she was
still modestly covered by her gown, he froze. "Sorry."

"Brent," she admonished, smiling. "It's okay."

"Okay," he breathed, smiling back. "I'll be in the living
room, if you need anything. So, uh . . . good luck."

"Thanks." She looked gratefully up at him.

"Anytime." He winked, and she watched as he strode
across the room and gently clicked the door shut behind
him.

Much to her amazement, Brent's reporterlike attention to
detail in class proved invaluable, and Meg proceeded to fill
her tummy with gusto. "He's pretty cool, huh?" Elaine
asked the busily feeding baby. "He says it's okay if you want
to call him Daddy someday. Isn't that neat? You'll learn to
love him," she whispered confidentially. "I did."

The fire Brent had laid earlier that evening crackled mer-
rily in the fireplace, casting a warm glow across the living
room. Elaine stretched contentedly and snuggled into the
corner of her sofa, enjoying the peaceful moments of solitude while Brent put Meg down for the night. The weeks
since the baby's birth had passed in a foggy haze of night
feedings and diaper changes for Elaine, as she adjusted to
her new life. And, much to her disbelief, she was loving
every minute of motherhood. Thanks to Brent.

He'd been so wonderful. Each night after work he'd come
home and taken care of the baby, handling her with the skill
of a seasoned father. Watching him in action never ceased
to bring a lump of joy to her throat. And after Meg had
gone to bed each evening, he would regale her with tales
from the office, keeping her in touch with the goings on. It
still surprised her how little she thought about, or missed,
the station. She was quite content to stay home and nurture

her daughter and enjoy Brent's company. Soon enough she would have to return to the daily grind.

They never seemed to run out of things to talk about, though the conversation—thankfully—revolved mostly around Meg's brilliant achievements. Elaine carefully avoided discussing their relationship for fear she might blurt out her innermost feelings toward him and drive him screaming out the door.

Her eyes glazed over as she stared at the dancing flames. Her contentment was marred only by the niggling doubts she had, concerning the feelings she was forming for Brent. And, on the rare occasion that she could bring herself to face the facts, she worried about the unbreakable bond that had formed between him and the baby, as well. Both mother and child were beginning to need and depend on him so much, Elaine dreaded the day when he would pack up his sleeping bag and head back to his cluttered apartment.

How could she ever return to her old life? She couldn't imagine. Not after having sampled the heaven of family. Her eyes shifted from the fire to the Christmas tree Brent had brought home after Thanksgiving last week. He was so thoughtful. Someday he would make some lucky woman a wonderful husband. The thought was completely and utterly depressing.

How on earth had this happened? Just last year at this time, she was telling Sara that she couldn't even begin to understand her intense desire for a family, and now, well, now she could understand perfectly.

Suddenly she wished she could discuss her predicament with her sweet, sympathetic cousin. Elaine missed her desperately. The yawning chasm Sara had left in her heart was slowly being filled by her daughter and Brent, but the scar would be with her always.

"She's sound asleep."

Pulling her focus from the fire, she turned to smile at Brent as he flopped down on the couch beside her. "I'm glad,'' she murmured sleepily. ''We had a long day today. I'm tired.''

Brent lifted his feet to her coffee table and, shoving a stack of magazines to the floor, made himself comfortable. It continued to confound her that his slovenly housekeeping habits didn't matter to her. She'd certainly changed. For some reason she found his messy little quirks endearing. Her priorities were so different now, sometimes she barely recognized herself.

''You look sleepy,'' he commented, thoughtfully studying her face. ''How are you feeling these days, anyway?''

''Terrific. Back to normal, pretty much. I won't be doing any gymnastics in the near future,'' she teased, ''but cartwheels never really were my forte.''

''You certainly have bounced back quickly,'' he noted approvingly. ''No one would ever be able to guess you gave birth just over a month ago.''

She was inordinately pleased that he'd noticed. Smiling modestly, she said, ''I'm doing okay, for an old broad.''

He shook his head and laughed. ''You're not old.''

''Maybe, but if I don't get to bed soon, I'll fall asleep right here on the couch. Ten years ago, I could easily stay up all night long, but these days...'' She sighed. ''Well, anyway, you have to get up early, and I'm sitting on your bed,'' she paused awkwardly, suddenly aware that she was indeed sitting on his bed. Saying it out loud seemed incredibly intimate, and with his uncanny ability to read her thoughts, she decided she'd better get out of there. ''So, uh, good night.''

Their eyes collided and locked. She could tell he hadn't missed the reference to his bed, or her apparent uneasiness about being there with him at this late hour. The look she encountered in the deep recesses of his dark green gaze sent a rush of new and unexpected feelings coursing through her. Feelings of desire and longing. For the first time in her life, Elaine was beginning to understand what it meant to be completely in love, and her heart pounded wildly with exhilaration. He was able to make her feel so feminine. Not at all the barracuda she knew the rest of the news crew saw her to be.

Standing on unsteady legs, she tried to appear nonchalant. "Good night," she said airily, and before she could say anything further that would undoubtedly humiliate her, she headed for the safety of her room.

The tiny mewling of Meg's nighttime cry finally penetrated the pleasant dreams that flitted through Elaine's subconscious. Dreams of Brent and white picket fences and loving all the time. And more babies that looked like Meg and Brent. Struggling back to wakefulness from the elusive Shangri-la of her dreams, she sat up, pulled on her robe and, standing slowly, proceeded to stagger to the nursery.

But the nursery was empty. Confused, Elaine left the baby's room and made her way to the living room, where she paused at the doorway and took in the poignant scene before her.

Brent, clad only in a pair of loose-fitting pajama bottoms, held little Meg against the powerful wall of his bare chest and walked slowly around the room, babbling to her in tender baby talk. She stood, drinking in the sight for a moment, amazed at how his imposing physique contrasted with the fragile babe in his arms. It was so unbelievably sweet.

She cleared her throat slightly, to make her presence known, and he looked up at her and smiled a smile that sent shock waves through her heart. How could she have been so blind where he was concerned? She'd actually managed to convince herself that this hunk of a man was nothing but a hick from the sticks.

He was anything but that. Brent Clark was a man among men. No wonder everyone in the secretarial pool was enamored of him. He was not only the nicest man she'd ever met, but he was also stunningly gorgeous. She shivered, reacting to the raw, animal magnetism that was palpable from clear across the room.

"She just needed a change, I think," he whispered, moving toward her through the flickering shadows that emanated from the fireplace. "I didn't want to wake you, considering how tired you've been." Tucking his chin to his chest, he smiled at the baby's cherubic face. "I was just going to put her down."

Elaine could only nod, too overcome by the need that had sprung to life deep in the well-guarded recesses of her soul, and followed him numbly to the nursery. Standing next to him as he lowered the baby into her crib and tucked her in, she knew that she should go back to her room. He had everything under control here. But try as she might, she couldn't seem to make her heart obey the dictates of her mind. She stood helplessly as he finished his task and turned to look at her.

And, convincing her once and for all that he could truly read her mind, he slowly reached out and pulled her into his arms.

Chapter Nine

Brent gathered her body up against his, and Elaine was filled with a breathless wonderment at the raw power of his embrace. Running her fingertips over the heated curves of his well-muscled, delightfully bare chest, she suddenly knew that she hadn't even begun to realize how much she'd craved his touch. Elaine caught her breath as he eased them down into the rocker and cradled her in his lap. The slow, rocking sensation, coupled with the breathtaking kisses he rained across her cheeks before returning to her mouth, was the most erotic experience she'd ever had.

The day that Brent had moved in with her, she'd per- suaded herself that there would be no problem keeping their relationship strictly platonic. After all, he was far too level- headed to become involved with a hormonal basket case like herself. Not to mention the fact that she was also his boss. The kisses they had shared before he'd moved in had merely been a reaction to the nightmares she'd endured at the loss of Sara and Bobby. His embrace had been a healing balm to her battered soul, and she had known instinctively that she could trust him.

But could she trust herself?

It was becoming increasingly clear that the answer to that question was no.

His kiss was gentle, but it was evident by his tortured touch, that he was exercising restraint. And when she didn't resist his advances, but instead, responded to him with abandon, he yielded to temptation and gave in to the lure of their passion. His kiss deepened with an urgency that sent shock waves of need down her spine and into her stomach.

Elaine's pulse was a raging timpani against her breast. Never before had she seen such a special look in a man's eyes. A look that told her how infinitely desirable she was to him. A look that told her without words just how badly he wanted her. And his increasing fervor ignited a matching blaze in her.

After all they'd been through together, bringing Meg into the world and learning to love her, being here with Brent this way seemed the most natural thing in the world. She didn't stop to analyze. She wanted him, and nothing had ever felt so right.

Their kiss was ardent, feverish in its intensity, driving Elaine half out of her mind from need. His mouth fitted hers oh, so exquisitely. She loved the sensation of his mustache as it tickled her upper lip, her neck and that special spot behind her ear.

His mustache suited his face, too, she decided woozily, running her hands through the ebony curls at the nape of his neck. It gave him a rugged, masculine look. And as his hands traveled up over her hips to her waist and then higher still, she felt goose bumps of pleasure rise over her entire body. She grasped his steel biceps for support and shivered.

He whispered words of need and encouragement along her lips, into her ears, against her neck. Arching back in his arms to give him access to the place where her throat blended into her collarbone, she sighed as she attempted to satisfy her voracious craving for the man who held the key to her heart.

He paused for a moment, looking down at her, his eyes filled with such eloquence, it threatened to undo the last shred of her composure. In that moment Elaine became lost in the rapture of the virile man who held the power to steal her heart. And it was thrilling. Intoxicating. Exhilarating. Like nothing she'd ever experienced before.

Dragging his lips from hers, his voice was ragged and husky as he spoke. "Elaine, I think we should . . ."

He stopped abruptly at Meg's cry, and Elaine felt as if someone had tossed a bucket of cold water over them.

He groaned and kissed her hard one last time. "She sounds hungry," he said. Releasing Elaine from his grasp, he nudged her—dazed—to her feet. "I'm sorry," he said, and standing up beside her, raked an unsteady hand across his jaw. "I never meant for it to go that far."

Meg's cry escalated.

"Of course," she said, suddenly confused, unable to meet his penetrating gaze. *He never meant for it to go that far.* She wrestled for an instant with the meaning of those words. Words that seared so painfully through her heart she was unable to speak. Obviously she'd misinterpreted the look in his eyes. Assigned a deeper meaning. She could only conclude that he'd never really wanted her in that way, but instead had fallen victim once again to her neediness. For him it had been a mistake. Purely physical. She felt like a charity case. "Me, too," she agreed, because her pride prevented her from doing otherwise.

He stood uncertainly for a moment, as though trying to decide what he could do to put things back to rights.

Still reeling from the powerful effects of his passion, Elaine moved woodenly to the crib and bent to lift the baby into her arms. Meg was so warm and cuddly, but even the child's cherubic presence couldn't fill the aching void that suddenly threatened to tear her heart in two.

He'd never meant for it to go that far. Of course. She'd known that from the beginning. How had she managed to make him an accomplice in her pathetic vacuum of a life? Obviously she'd taken unfair advantage of the fact that he felt sorry for her.

Mortified at having coerced him into filling her endless list of needs, she clutched the innocent baby tightly in her arms and managed a weak smile.

"I'll...feed her...now," she told him haltingly, wondering how she'd ever be able to face him in the morning. But she knew she would have to find a way. She would rally. Go on as if nothing unusual had happened. She was after all, Elaine Lewis, tough-as-nails television producer. It was time to remember that. She sighed, knowing deep in her heart that it was no longer true. She wasn't the same woman anymore. Not the same at all.

Forcing herself to return his tentative smile, she watched in despair as he backed out of the room.

Brent sagged into the couch that had been his bed since the baby had been born and stared despondently into the fire. Never had a woman affected him the way Elaine did. He'd been around the relationship block a time or two in his life, but never with the intensity that he had with Elaine. And yet, he thought, closing his eyes in disgust, he'd nearly blown it just now. Nearly given in to the unbearable temptation to claim her as his own. To show her physically just what she'd come to mean to him.

What a clod. Wincing, he allowed his head to drop back against the back of the couch. What the hell had he been thinking? The woman had just given birth for crying out loud. The last thing he was sure she wanted at this point was to be pawed by a lust-crazed employee.

Except it wasn't lust. Groaning, he pulled one of her afghans across his bare torso. It was love. He loved Elaine Lewis with every fiber of his being, and he was dying to show her. But he couldn't. Not now. She was still in mourning. Still healing mentally and physically from events she'd had no control over.

Oh, damn. He pummeled a needlepoint throw pillow and called himself every kind of fool. He'd really mucked it up back there, too. He'd wanted to make her understand how profoundly sorry he was that he'd taken advantage of the situation. To tell her that he understood how she felt, and what she was going through. To tell her that he loved her, but if she didn't return his feelings, that it was okay. He understood.

But no. Instead, he'd blurted out some gibberish about not wanting to go that far. What the hell did that mean? It was obvious that she'd been confused. Although, much to her credit, she'd been gracious and let him off the hook. He was probably lucky she didn't slap the living daylights out of him.

Balling the throw pillow up into a mangled wad, he made a vow, right there and then, that no matter how desperately he wanted her, he would wait until she was ready. No more physical contact. It would be torture, but then again, another incomplete encounter like the one in the nursery, just now, might possibly kill him.

In the meantime, he would become so indispensable to her that she couldn't envision life without him. And when he asked her to marry him, she wouldn't be able to refuse. Unless, of course, he'd blown it. If that was the case, he'd join a monastery, because life as he'd known it before Elaine was over.

Two weeks later the classroom at Chicago Central Hospital was decorated festively for Christmas. Everyone from the birth class was there to show off their new offspring, and Elaine and Brent were no exception.

Cornered at the punch bowl by the new mothers in the group, Elaine did her best to follow the conversation and at the same time keep an eye on her small family. Poor Brent stood at the other end of the room cradling Meg in his arms, held captive by Dick Olsen's incessant sales pitch. She felt sorry for him, and as soon as she got a chance, decided to rush over and rescue him.

Smiling, she caught his eye. He nodded imperceptibly in her direction, and without a word made it clear that the sooner she could come to his aid the better.

"Your husband sure is a proud papa," Dick's wife, Mary, said, nibbling on a Christmas cookie and following Elaine's gaze across the room. She shifted her son in her arms and inclined her head at Brent.

Liz Martin turned slightly to see what they were talking about. "He's really cute with her," she commented in agreement. "So protective. It's amazing how much Meg takes after him. You must hear that a lot."

Squinting, Elaine thoughtfully studied Brent and her baby. They were right. Meg's downy curls were the same dark shade, her eyes held the same sweet countenance, even her nose and chin were replicas in feminine form of Brent's. It was pretty uncanny. Funny how she'd never noticed that before.

"One of the nurses at the hospital mentioned that, just after she was born," Elaine said, remembering Sandy's remark. And though she knew it was impossible, it pleased her that everyone seemed to think that Brent really was Meg's father. In a way he was. Although she knew that no amount of wishing on her part could make it permanent. She would just have to enjoy these brief months of maternity leave together while she could. Then Brent would move on and leave her and the baby to face the world alone. Just like everyone else in her life.

This dismal train of thought didn't bear thinking about, she mentally chided herself. It was a party, for heaven's sake. She would just have to cross that bridge when she came to it. Too bad she couldn't blow the bridge up.

Mary's smile was shy. "I can see why the nurse would say that. They are two of a kind, aren't they?" She reached over and helped herself to several more cookies. "I don't think our boy looks like either of us. You're lucky, Elaine," she offered bashfully. "You and Brent are such a stunning couple, Meg is sure to be a beauty."

Taken aback, Elaine was at a total loss for words. *Stunning couple?* It was true that Brent looked quite handsome tonight in his faded jeans and cowboy boots. The casual shirt he wore was pressed for once, thanks to her. He wore it opened slightly at the collar, and the sleeves were rolled up revealing his strong forearms. His straight white teeth flashed beneath his dark mustache as an easy, tolerant grin stole across his face from time to time. He stood, his legs spread slightly for balance and rocked the baby back and forth as he patiently listened to Dick's endless diatribe. No wonder every woman he came in contact with fell in love with him.

Liz sighed. "I wish Danny would take half the interest in Harmony that Brent does in Meg." Pausing, she untangled Harmony's chubby fist from her long, ruler-straight hair. "Brent is so natural with her. Danny claims he's afraid of breaking Harmony. I think it's just an excuse to hide in the garage and work on his bike," she said confidentially.

Young Vicky jostled her squalling son in her arms, absorbing the conversation of the older mothers. "If you think that's bad, you should try living with a guy who works two jobs during the day and goes to school at night. I'm stuck with Trevor all by myself every day. None of my friends want to hang around us anymore, and I'm afraid that Jason is just going to take off someday, like his dad did to him."

The fear that flashed across her youthful face tore at Elaine's heart. In some ways she could identify with the girl.

Vicky looked over at Jason, who stood alone and visibly uncomfortable by the door. "I think you guys are lucky." She patted the fussy Trevor on his back. "Especially you." Vicky grinned up at Elaine. "He's cool," she pronounced, referring to Brent with all the wisdom of a teenage groupie.

"Yes." Elaine had to agree. He was very cool. Deciding that this was the perfect opportunity to make good her escape, Elaine excused herself from the gathering at the refreshment table and moved across the room toward Brent.

"I brought you some punch," she said, smiling as she extricated him from Dick's clutches and led him to a deserted section of the room where they could talk for a moment. Ever since the night of their fateful kiss in the nursery two weeks ago, they'd been somewhat formal with each other. Elaine hated that fact that their easy camaraderie was a thing of the past, and hoped that Brent's festive mood could help them get beyond that, for tonight at least. It seemed she was in luck.

"Thanks," he breathed, taking the cup of punch from her hand. "Dick had such a tight grip on my arm, I was afraid I was going to have to chew it off at the shoulder to get away."

Elaine laughed gleefully, drawing looks of envy from the other wives in the party. "He can be tenacious."

Brent snorted. "No lie. Did you know that we need a family car immediately? He wants us to come out to the lot tomorrow."

"What'd you say?"

"Shecky, get the jet."

They laughed, finally easy with each other again.

"Just kidding. I told him I had to talk to the little woman." He grinned at her. "It's not a bad idea, really. Your Jag isn't really made for family life, and I can't keep stealing the company van."

"True," Elaine agreed, "but do you think we should go to Dick?"

"Not without a bodyguard." His eyes twinkled pleasantly. "He's pretty upset that Mary hasn't lost any weight since the baby was born."

"What a creep," Elaine said, and smiled in greeting across the room at the Harlows in their matching red-and-green sweatsuits. Even Harlow, Jr., sported a tiny red-and-green sleeper. They looked festive. In a way she envied their corny little family.

"Yeah. Says she's still sleeping in the spare room." Brent wiggled his eyebrows, his expression loaded with meaning.

"Can you blame her?"

Brent shook his head. "No. He did want to know, however, if we were...uh, you know, back in the saddle, so to speak."

Elaine gasped and then giggled nervously. "What did you say?"

"I told him not for lack of trying."

"Brent!"

"What?" He feigned innocence. "I think he has a crush on you. He couldn't get over how fetching you look in this outfit." He tugged playfully on the sleeve of her red pant-suit. "He's right, you know. You are definitely the best looking woman in the room."

"Oh, for crying out loud..." Elaine huffed, knowing that he was teasing her, and loving it. Luckily, before their conversation could grow any more awkward, Nurse Shocktaag came over to make the obligatory party talk.

Ruby stared down her pointed nose at Meg, who stared back apprehensively at this new face. This was not Mommy or Daddy, her look seemed to say.

"Hello, little one." Ruby tickled her under the chin, and Meg smiled. "How are you liking your mother and father? Are they being good to you?"

"Brrbbtt." Meg drooled and blew bubbles.

"Ah, so you like them, no? This is good. I can tell they like you very much, too. You are daddy's princess?"

Meg waved her arms and squealed.

"Yes." The stern woman pursed her lips and winked knowingly at the baby. "I can see the bond. There is nothing like daddy to make us feel safe."

Brent smiled over the top of the baby's head at Elaine, and longing to linger in the delightful glow of this fairy tale, she smiled back.

* * *

"Hey. You're supposed to be asleep," Brent whispered to Meg, as he peered down into her crib at her. Lifting her up to his broad shoulder, he moved through the moonlight and settled with her in the rocker. Unable to drift off to sleep after the party, he'd decided to check on the baby. He was feeling decidedly restless. Elaine had looked so beautiful tonight. She stirred something in his gut that he was beginning to fear would never go away.

"So, what did you think of all those other babies tonight?" he asked the child who nestled securely against his chest. "They were kind of lame compared to you, huh? You were definitely the smartest kid in the bunch." He patted her back. "And," he murmured in quiet baby talk, loving the way she stared so contentedly up at him, "you is definitely the prettiest one, too. Just like mama."

He hummed a few bars of a lullaby from one of the tapes Elaine had bought, and her eyes began to drift shut as he rocked her back and forth. "You know," he whispered. "I wish you really were my little girl. I feel like your daddy already." Her eyes shut tight, and she gripped a lock of his hair in her tiny fist, melting his heart.

"I promise you, little one. I'm going to do everything in my power to convince your mama that she needs to marry me someday." He paused and stroked her soft curls with his finger. "I just have to figure out how I'm going to do it, that's all. I have to make her an offer she can't refuse."

He continued murmuring sweet nothings about a future together as the moon slowly rose in the winter sky. A future of Christmases and Birthdays, a future of bicycles and roller skates, a future of brothers and sisters who were as smart and beautiful as she and her mother were.

The next morning Elaine turned off the shower's rejuvenating spray and stood listening. It was quiet. Good. The baby hadn't awakened yet. She'd become quite adept at jumping in and out of the shower while the baby slept, all the while listening for her tiny cry.

As she stood toweling off, a sound reached her ears, but it wasn't the sound she'd been anticipating. It was the doorbell. Hurriedly, she reached to the back of the bathroom door for her robe and wondered who on earth it could be. Brent had left for work over an hour ago.

Wrapping the sash firmly around her waist, she twisted a fluffy bath towel around her head, and after a quick peek into the nursery at the still-sleeping Meg, went to see who would be calling at this hour of the morning.

She peered though the peephole and discovered an elegantly dressed, highly sophisticated-looking woman standing impatiently on her stoop. Elaine didn't recognize her, but deciding that she most likely wasn't here to rob the place, pulled open her front door and smiled a curious greeting.

"Hello." The regal woman's smile was polished. "I don't believe we've met. I'm looking for an Elaine Lewis?" She extended a perfectly manicured hand. "I'm Amanda Johnson. Bobby Johnson's mother."

Chapter Ten

"**O**h." Flustered, Elaine grasped the proffered hand for a moment as a feeling of foreboding washed over her. Bobby's mother. Of course. She'd heard about her from Sara on occasion, but knew that there had been a certain amount of estrangement between the young couple and this intimidating woman. With the emotional upheaval of the past year, Elaine hadn't given much thought to Amanda Johnson, other than to wonder briefly why she hadn't attended her son's funeral.

"Won't you please come in?" she asked, self-consciously smoothing the towel that adorned her head.

Nodding confidently, Amanda brushed past Elaine, as a cloud of cloying, expensive perfume wafted after her into the foyer.

"Please, uh—come this way," Elaine invited awkwardly, leading Amanda to the living room and wishing she'd had a chance to straighten up. Brent's sleeping bag lay in a rumpled pile on the floor next to the couch, and his personal effects were strewn about in his typical happy-go-lucky style. The chaos hadn't bothered her until now.

Quickly shoving his bedding aside and tossing his dirty laundry into a pile in the corner, she turned and sent a flushed smile in her visitor's direction. "Please—" she gestured to the couch "—have a seat."

"Thank you," Amanda murmured, glancing disdainfully around the cluttered room.

It was obvious from the look on her face that she disapproved of Elaine's housekeeping abilities. Swallowing her embarrassment, Elaine tightened the sash to her robe and racked her brain to remember what Sara had told her about Bobby's mother.

Bits and pieces of previous conversations with her cousin flashed through her mind as she tried to organize what precious little she knew about the woman.

Amanda Johnson had never been much of a mother-in-law, as Elaine recalled. Always on the go, the socialite had made a career of seeing the world after her husband and Bobby's father—Robert Johnson, Sr.—had passed away several years ago.

Sara, bless her compassionate heart, had felt it was Amanda's way of dealing with the grief of losing her husband. To run away from it. She had defended Amanda's continued absence by saying that she was sure Bobby's mother would return to her home in Chicago as soon as she and Bobby presented her with a grandchild. Sara had loved the idea of a big family—complete with doting grandmother—no matter how spoiled its members were. And Sara had believed that if there was one thing in this world Amanda loved more than spending money and traveling, it was her only son. She would return soon, Sara had predicted, just wait and see.

Elaine had had a feeling her cousin had been suffering from a severe case of denial, considering Amanda had been conspicuously absent from their wedding, but Elaine had felt, if it made Sara happy to hope for the best, then so be it.

Unfortunately Elaine's feelings had not been unfounded. One day shortly after Robert passed away, Bobby had confided the truth to Elaine. And the truth of the matter had been that Amanda hadn't felt that Sara was in her son's league socially and had continually urged him to leave his young wife. Especially since the poor thing had been unable to bear him an heir. After a bitter argument, Amanda had stormed off to Europe, and as far as Elaine knew, never had the chance to make amends with her precious son. Beyond that, there was little else Elaine knew about Amanda.

Other than the fact that the woman was turning her into a nervous wreck at the moment. Fidgeting under her scrutiny, she wished that Amanda would stop staring at the towel she wore turban-style around her head and state her business.

"What can I do for you?" Elaine asked politely, trying to quell the disquieting feeling of doom that had followed Amanda into her home.

Amanda settled gingerly into her seat, crossed her long, shapely stocking-clad legs and smiled rigidly. "It is my understanding that you are Sara Johnson's first cousin."

Elaine nodded and wondered how appropriate it would be to offer condolences about the young couple to Amanda, considering the nature of her relationship with Bobby at the time of his death. She decided to wait and let his mother set the tone.

"Yes, that's true. Our mothers were sisters. When her parents passed on, she came to live with my folks until she married your son," she said. Adrenaline flowed through her veins, and she felt her body reacting instinctively to this perceived enemy. Although she couldn't quite put her finger on the problem, she could sense something was wrong. Very wrong.

Reaching into her small clutch bag, Amanda withdrew a packet of what appeared to be paperwork of some kind and then sat back in her chair and looked directly at Elaine.

"It is also my understanding that you were close to my son and his wife." It was more of a statement than a question. Elaine's radar clicked into overdrive as she wondered where the woman was leading with this.

"Yes. I loved them both very much."

What could have been a flash of pain briefly touched Amanda's eyes. "Yes." She nodded. "Then I'm sure you are aware that Bobby and I were very close until he decided to marry Sara."

"Uh," Elaine wet her dry lips with her tongue.

"It's all right." Amanda waved a dismissive hand in her direction. "He never did listen to me." Her face softened for a moment. "It's no secret that I felt he married beneath his social class. No offense," she hastened to loftily assure Elaine.

Insulted Elaine arched an eyebrow, tightening her grip on the arm of her chair.

"You are probably also aware," she continued, "that Bobby and I had a ... falling out ... before I left for France last year."

Noticing the visible anguish that tinged Amanda's cultured voice, Elaine nodded. Now that she was a mother herself, she could only imagine what it must be like to lose a child after a quarrel. She could almost feel sorry for the woman. Almost, but not quite.

"I did not learn of his death until after the funeral." Amanda's eyes glazed over. "His lawyer went to a considerable amount of trouble to find me, but by then it was too late. Bobby was gone." She sighed and shook her head as if to clear it from the demons that tormented her over the rift with her son. "I saw no point in coming home to a lot of unhappy memories, so I stayed in France with some old family friends and dealt with my grief." Her laugh was short and derisive. "There was no one left to come home to, anyway."

"I'm so sorry for your loss," Elaine murmured, uncomfortable with the personal nature of the conversation. For the life of her, Elaine couldn't figure out why Bobby's mother was here, telling her such confidences. And why now? She wriggled restlessly in her seat.

"I am, too." Amanda glanced down at the papers she held in her hands. "That brings me to why I'm here."

"Oh?" Finally. Dread filled her heart as she waited for the other shoe to drop.

"Yes. When I came home, I found some papers in my son's safe-deposit box. I contacted his lawyer and discussed them with him."

Elaine's eyes darted to Amanda's as the tiny hairs at the back of her neck stood at attention. *What papers?* she wondered anxiously.

Smiling and confident, Bobby's mother held the packet up for Elaine to see. "I was surprised to learn that you had entered into an agreement with my son and daughter-in-law to act as a surrogate mother for their child. I knew that they were exploring that option. At one point I think Sara even considered me." Her condescending smile was hard, and it was evident that she thought the very idea was ridiculous.

Elaine bristled. She probably didn't want to ruin her perfect figure, she thought uncharitably. Age certainly couldn't have been an issue. Platinum blond and wrinkle free, Amanda hardly looked old enough to be Bobby's mother.

It suddenly dawned on Elaine that some other woman could have given birth to Meg, and the thought was immensely disturbing. She couldn't envision Amanda as anybody's mother, let alone sweet, innocent little Meg. Never had she been more delighted than she was now, that she had agreed to give life to the baby. Besides Brent, it was the most wonderful, miraculous thing that had ever happened to her. No job or perfectly toned figure could ever give her the happiness she had now, thanks to her new little family. She doubted that someone like Amanda could ever understand that.

"Anyway, being that this child would be my granddaughter or grandson," Amanda continued, "I wanted to find out if anything had ever come of this agreement, and if so—" she eyed Elaine coolly "—I would like to file for adoption."

Adoption? Suddenly Elaine felt faint and her heart leapt into her throat. Dear Lord. This unfeeling, emotionless woman wanted to take her child from her? No! Every maternal instinct ever known to womankind sprang to life within Elaine as she felt herself tense for battle. Never. The only way this woman would ever get Meg was over her dead body.

Her mind reeled frantically. What would she do? Lie. Yes, that was it, she would tell the woman that there had never been a baby. Then, hopefully, Amanda would go away, back to some foreign country and leave them alone.

She opened her mouth to speak, but unfortunately Meg had other ideas and chose that moment to announce her existence to her grandmother.

Amanda's eyes widened with interest as she homed in on the cries that came from the nursery. "Is that the baby?" she asked, unable to contain her curiosity. "May I see him?"

No! Elaine wanted to scream. Grandmother or not, this woman couldn't just waltz in here and announce that she wanted to take her baby. Valiantly she struggled to understand the strain the woman must be under. To give her the benefit of the doubt. Perhaps she didn't really mean what she was saying. Perhaps it was just the grief talking. "Her," Elaine duly informed her. "It's a girl."

"A girl?" Shrugging off her disappointment, Amanda rose to her feet and followed the sound of Meg's voice.

Taken aback by her bold behavior, Elaine rushed after and found the woman standing next to the crib. Amanda's perfectly manicured hand was covering her mouth and her eyes glistened with unshed tears.

"She's beautiful," she breathed, sorrow at all she had missed out on these past few years with her son filling her expression.

"Yes," Elaine agreed, apprehensively. "She is."

Amanda stood, staring at her granddaughter for a moment, then turned abruptly and left the room. Elaine picked up the fussy baby and held her tightly to her breast. She kissed Meg's sunny little face and whispered words of comfort and reassurance as she followed the baby's grandmother back to the living room on unsteady legs. Trying to rein in her runaway emotions, she patted the child's bottom and longed for Brent's comforting presence. He would know what to do with this . . . this . . . barracuda.

"I want her," Amanda announced without preamble. "I want to adopt her. She is all that I have left of my son."

She turned to confront Elaine. The cold, calculating look that crossed Amanda's face sent waves of terror rippling through her body. Gripping Meg so tightly that the child squeaked in protest, Elaine gallantly battled the hysterical urge to bolt.

"I imagine," Amanda continued, getting down to brass tacks, "since you are not the baby's biological mother, that you will be relieved to dispense of the burden of raising someone else's child. Since you are merely the surrogate, I feel that—as the child's grandmother—I have more of an emotional investment."

Elaine gasped, too shocked to respond to the woman's harsh words. "No," she whispered. When it came to emotional investment, she doubted that Amanda had a clue. Otherwise, she would leave the baby where she was.

"No?" Amanda's eyes narrowed. "Surely you can't mean that. It says right here," she waved the legal documents in her hand under Elaine's nose, "that you were planning to give the baby to Bobby. It say's right here in black and white that you wanted to make sure that your responsibility for the baby ended with the birth. Well—'' her tight laughter tin-kled sharply ''—I'm here to take over.''

Elaine longed to slap the smug look off the audacious woman's face. It had been a lifetime since she'd signed those papers. She was not the same woman who'd agreed to that arrangement a year ago. She was a mother now. And, like a she bear protecting her cub, she squared her shoulders in outrage.

''Mrs. Johnson, having just discovered the existence of the child, I don't believe you've had time to give this matter much thought,'' she said, her voice amazingly calm under the circumstances. ''I'm sure once you have taken time to consider all that would be involved with raising this child, you'll agree that she is better off with me. I'm the only mother she has ever known. And,'' she continued, her voice vehement, ''I want it to stay that way.''

''Oh, but you're wrong,'' Bobby's mother bit out tersely. ''I have given this a lot of thought. This is my chance to make amends to my son. By caring for his child. I can give the baby everything. I have money. I'm also going to be re-married this spring and can offer the child a father. My sources tell me that you are a single parent. What do you have to offer?'' She glanced around at Elaine's messy house in disgust.

Shaking with rage, Elaine leveled her gaze at the regal woman. ''Love,'' she said, her tone protective—deadly. ''I can offer her love.''

And that was something she felt quite sure that Amanda was in short supply of. Taking the baby because of some misplaced sense of guilt over a bad relationship with her first child certainly wouldn't do anybody any good.

Marching over to her front door, she yanked it open and inclined her head toward her unwelcome visitor. ''I'll thank you kindly to leave now.''

''Certainly.'' Amanda seemed unfazed. ''You'll be hear-ing from my lawyer in the next few days. You haven't heard the last of this," she promised, before stepping arrogantly to the porch.

Slamming the door behind her, Elaine sagged with the baby against its solid surface long enough to gather her wits, swallow the giant obstruction in her throat and blink away the tears that blinded her. *How dare she?* she raged, shifting Meg to a more comfortable position on her shoulder. *Never. Not in a million years.* Not even if she had to pack the baby up and move to outer Mongolia would she let that evil woman get her clutches on this child.

Striding back to the nursery, she laid the baby back down in her crib, then rushed to the phone to call Brent at work. Her fingers shook violently as she dialed the number. Taking several deep breaths to calm her shattered nerves, she knew that everything would be all right once she could hear Brent's voice. It always was.

"Oh, thank God!" Elaine breathed, and practically dragged the bewildered Brent into her house.

His eyes darted quickly around the foyer, worriedly looking for signs of trouble. "I got here as quickly as I could. What's going on? Is everything all right? Where is the baby?" he asked, fear unlike any he'd ever experienced before clawing at his throat. Elaine's frantic phone call had scared the hell out of him. He'd broken land speed records to get here, and now, seeing her tear-stained face, he felt his alarm begin to rise.

Grasping tight fistfuls of his jacket in her shaking hands, she looked miserably up at him and tried to speak. "She wants to take her away," she whispered, her anguished face pale. She was quivering like an aspen leaf.

"Who?" Brent framed her face between his hands and tilted it up to his. "Who wants to take who away?"

Elaine touched her tongue to her lower lip and closed her eyes. "Amanda Johnson. She wants to take Meg. Brent, she can't do this to us. It's Christmas next week," she added.

He cut her off. "What?" Brent stiffened. His stomach felt as though it had sunk clear to his shoes, and his heart stood still. Someone wanted to take Meg away? "Who's Amanda Johnson? Where is Meg?" The muscles worked convulsively in his jaw.

"She's asleep in the nursery." Elaine choked on a sob and lifted her tear-spiked lashes up to Brent. "She's taking her morning nap. Oh, Brent, she always takes her nap at this time every morning," she babbled, panic-stricken. "I know that. I'm her mother. No one else can ever care for her the way I can."

"Of course you're her mother," he said soothingly. Drawing her into his embrace he wondered what the devil she was getting at. He held her tightly for a moment then, taking her hands in his, he lead her to the living room and pulled her down next to him on the couch. "Why don't you tell me what's going on?" he instructed, trying to slow his own raging pulse. "Start at the beginning. Who is this Amanda Johnson?"

He sat on pins and needles, waiting for her to organize her muddled thoughts. She looked as if she'd seen a ghost, her anxiety was palpable.

"Amanda Johnson is Bobby's mother."

"Meg's father, Bobby?"

"Yes. She's Meg's biological grandmother. She wants to adopt Meg."

Brent sat stupefied as he tried to reconcile the meaning of Elaine's words. He couldn't believe it. He wouldn't believe it. No one would ever take Meg away as long as he had a breath of life left in his body. He would fight this battle for Elaine, and he would win. Of that he was confident. But first he had to size up his opponent.

"Why now? Why has she waited so long to come forward? Why haven't you mentioned her to me before?"

Elaine drew a deep shuddering breath and wrapped her arms protectively around her middle. She looked so frail and lost, Brent suddenly wanted to tear this rotten Amanda woman limb from limb.

"She was in Europe at the time of Bobby's death. She claims that she only just now discovered our agreement in his safe-deposit box."

"What agreement?" Brent was puzzled.

Elaine reached over to the coffee table and picked up a sheaf of papers. "The surrogacy agreement I signed with Bobby and Sara. I told you about it before, remember?" Brent nodded as she handed him the document. "This is my copy. I dug it out of my files after Amanda left."

Brent took the papers from her hand and removed his reading glasses from his jacket pocket. Frowning, he positioned the glasses on his nose and began to scan the document as Elaine poured out the details of Amanda's visit.

He nodded absently from time to time, listening with half an ear. Something about this whole thing just didn't add up. The reporter's blood in him surged through his veins. The more Elaine talked, the more Amanda was beginning to sound like a case. Bobby, on the other hand, sounded like a smart guy. Surely anyone with half a brain would know his mother might try to undermine this surrogacy project. Especially since it seemed that she disliked his young wife so much, he mused, scanning the document.

"Did you read this whole thing?" he asked Elaine, interrupting her tearful account of her unfortunate encounter with Bobby's mother.

"Um," she sniffed and her delicate brow furrowed together. "I think so. Most of it, anyway. I knew that Bobby and Sara would take care of me. I wasn't really that worried about the fine print."

"Mmm." Nodding, Brent ran his hand over his jaw. "Why?"

"I don't know," he admitted, flipping through the pages. "I just have a feeling. I can't explain it, but from what you tell me about Amanda and Bobby, I just...get...the idea ... that ..." his voice trailed off as he squinted thoughtfully at the last page.

"What?" Elaine leaned over his body and tried to see what he was reading with such rapt attention.

He looked up at her and, for the first time since he'd walked through the door, grinned. Then, he kissed her on the nose.

"What?" She glanced up from the paperwork to him in confusion.

"I think that good old Bobby was a pretty smart guy. I like the way he thinks."

"Why?"

"Because it says right here, that in the event of his and Sara's death, you are to be named the baby's parent."

"What?" Elaine squealed, delighted. Relief flooded her beautiful features, and she smiled brilliantly, stealing Brent's breath for a moment. "That's fabulous!"

"Well, yes, but there is one provision." Pulling his reading glasses off, Brent chewed thoughtfully on the stem.

"What provision. Where?" Elaine snatched the document out of his hands and searched it to find what he was talking about.

"At the bottom there." Brent pointed to the specific clause. "It would seem that you need to be ... married."

Chapter Eleven

"Oh, no," Elaine breathed, suddenly crestfallen. "That's terrible. I'm not married." Groaning, she pushed her hair away from her face and slumped dejectedly against Brent. "That must be why Amanda made a point of telling me that she was going to be remarried in the spring. Obviously Bobby wanted his child to have two parents."

Brent felt a surge of excitement rumble through his stomach. This could be just the opportunity he was looking for. If only he could convince Elaine.... He sat in silence for a moment, searching for a way to broach an idea that was beginning to form in his mind. He had to tread lightly. This was no time to scare her away. With a massive effort, he tried to swallow his zeal and appear nonchalant.

"I can see his point," he deadpanned, schooling his tone to reflect her agitation with this disappointing turn of events.

"But why?" she cried in frustration. "I'm a good mother."

"The best," he agreed. "But apparently, Bobby and Sara felt it was important that their baby have a father. They never discussed this with you?"

"No. I'm sure they never foresaw the need. How could they have known?"

"True," Brent mused, still trying to remain outwardly cool and at the same time keep from exploding with eagerness.

"What are we going to do?" Elaine was beginning to grow agitated again.

"I don't know," he said, frowning his thoughtful, reporter frown. "I suppose you could get married."

"Oh, sure," she sighed. "When they build a Tastee-Freez in hell. I haven't even been on a date in well over a year. Anyway, who would be crazy enough to marry someone who just had a baby?" She covered her face with her hands.

"It's not so crazy," Brent said offhandedly. "In fact, I can think of someone who'd be willing to help out."

"Oh, yeah? Who?" she asked through her fingers.

"Me."

Holding his breath, Brent watched her peel her hands away from the shocked expression on her face. *Please,* he prayed, *please don't say no.* Not yet.

Before she could object, he continued. "I've grown very fond of Meg. And her mother," he added, smiling, and reached out to pull her hands into his. "I'm probably as worried about Bobby's mother taking Meg away as you are. And considering it's my name listed as father on her birth certificate, who better to play the part?" He tightened his grip on her hands. "Elaine, marry me."

"Oh, Brent," Elaine whispered. "You don't have to do that. You've already done so much." Tears glistened in her eyes as she looked up into the face that had become so beautiful to her. This was the moment she'd come to dream about.

If she were honest with herself, she would have to admit that she wanted this more than she'd ever wanted anything else in her entire life. But how could she saddle him with even more responsibility? It didn't seem fair that he was constantly having to bail her out of every jam that came her way. Marriage was certainly above and beyond the call of duty for a reporter just doing his job. She doubted that Walter Cronkite would have gone this far just to get a story about childbirth.

The man was a saint. No wonder she loved him so much. But she would have to turn him down. It was only fair. When—and if—Brent ever proposed to her for real, she wanted it to be because he loved her and Meg as much as they'd come to love him. Then they could be the family of her dreams.

No. There had to be a better way.

"Elaine, if you won't do it for me, do it for Meg. We can't lose her. Not now. I don't think I could stand it." His steady gaze bore into her in silent challenge. "I want to be part of her life," he argued. "To teach her how to ride a bike. To interrogate her boyfriends when the time comes. To be there for her when she needs me."

She was beginning to melt. She must steel herself against her crazy impulse to give in to him. He didn't know what he was getting into.

Brent could tell she was waffling. He searched for a way to convince her that this was their only choice. "It could be a short-term agreement, if you like." Speaking quickly, he pulled out his trump card. He would give her an out. How could she resist such logic? "As soon as Amanda is taken care of, we could end the marriage...if you, you know... want to. We, uh, could figure that out later, of course." If it were up to him, the marriage wouldn't end until Willard Scott was wishing them happy record-breaking anniversary on national television.

Elaine felt an overwhelming wave of tenderness consume her at the vulnerable expression on his face. Never had she known anyone as wonderful as Brent Clark. And it was then that she knew—as much as she wanted to set him free to find his own happiness in life, she needed him.

Meg needed him.

The thought of losing the angel that slept so peacefully in the next room was more than she could bear. She wasn't strong enough to sustain yet another loss of a loved one. And that included Brent.

If he was sincere, she would love nothing more than to become Mrs. Elaine Clark. Maybe, after they were married, she could find a way to make Brent love her. She knew he already loved Meg.

"Are you sure?" She gulped hard; hot tears slipping unnoticed down her cheeks.

"More sure than I've ever been about anything else in my life."

"Okay, then." She sighed, as a tentative smile played at her lips. "Yes. I'll marry you."

Brent exhaled mightily in relief. Closing his eyes, he sent a prayer of thanksgiving heavenward, and then leaning forward, pulled Elaine into his arms to seal their agreement. As he lost himself in the shy, feather softness of her kiss, he knew that once she was legally his, he would find a way to make her love him.

"You're going to *what?* Brent, it sounded like you said you're going to get married," Margaret's incredulous voice squealed across the line from her living room in Iowa.

Brent grinned, envisioning the look of shock that his mother must be wearing. "You heard right, Mom. So instead of me coming home for Christmas this year, why don't you come to Chicago for the wedding and spend the holidays with us?"

Margaret was rendered speechless.

"Mom?"

"Yes, honey. I'm here. Who's the lucky woman?"

"Elaine."

"The pregnant one?"

Brent laughed. "She's not pregnant anymore, Mom," he reminded her. "We want to get married as soon as possible, so that we can spend the holidays as a family." It was a tiny fib, really. He and Elaine had agreed it would be wise to keep the nature of their agreement a secret. At least until Amanda called off the dogs. Then, if Elaine wanted, they could begin divorce proceedings. But he sure as hell wasn't going to bring it up. He'd never been happier in his life. He was getting the most beautiful, intelligent, sexy woman on the face of this earth, and an adorable baby daughter to boot. How could he be so fortunate?

"Mom, I just know you're going to love her," he promised. "We thought we'd get married next week on the Saturday before Christmas. I'm sending you an airline ticket today. You'll get here Friday afternoon, and you can stay at my place..." His voice trailed off as the sound of some pretty heavy sniffing and squeaking reached his ears.

"Mom? What's wrong?"

"Nothing, honey. It's just that I'm so happy."

"Me, too, Mom." Brent smiled into the phone. "Me, too."

The break room went silent. All eyes stared in shock at Brent. Finally, after what seemed like an eternity to him, Ray broke into an ear-splitting grin and slapped him on the back in a gesture of hearty congratulation.

"You old son of a gun. We all wondered what the deal was between you and The Barr—" Ray went suddenly pink "—uh, Elaine, but we never dreamed you'd fallen in love with her."

Brent grinned at the amazed expressions that had greeted the announcement of his impending nuptials to the boss. He only wished Elaine could have been here to enjoy their slack-jawed wonder, but she was busy making last-minute arrangements for the ceremony. For once he had the dubious distinction of being the one with the juiciest piece of gossip. He was sure he could have knocked most of them over with a feather. This should give them fodder for endless discussions about the particulars of Meg's paternity. He didn't care. As far as he was concerned, he was the baby's father.

"You're getting married Saturday?" Debbie asked, her gamin face scrunched into a knot of wonder. "*This* Saturday?"

"Yep." Brent nodded pleasantly and glanced around the table. "You're all invited, of course. It's going to be a small affair, just a few friends and family. The Old Church on Front Street, downtown. I know it's awfully close to Christmas, but if you could attend, it would mean a lot to both of us. We didn't really have time to have invitations printed or anything, so I'll send out a memo on the particulars."

"Wow. Congratulations," Stu offered with a grin. "Some people will do anything for a raise."

"Yeah," Debbie murmured, unable to keep the disappointment from her voice.

"I guess that means we won't be able to complain about her in front of you anymore, huh?" Ray joked, leaning back on his chair's hind legs, as the room began to buzz with the amazing news.

"'Fraid not." Brent winked at Debbie who smiled slowly in return, apparently deciding that if you can't beat 'em, join 'em.

"She's okay," she admitted grudgingly. "We had a nice talk at the hospital, and the baby—" Debbie beamed "—is a little doll. Good for you, Brent. I hope she'll be good to you."

"She's the best thing that ever happened to me," he told them. He only wished that Elaine felt the same way about him.

Considering that it had been a hastily planned, last-minute affair, the wedding was beautiful. Elaine made a radiant bride, dressed in a winter white tailored suit that accentuated her newly trim waistline and the soft curves of motherhood. The only thing that would have completed her delirious happiness was the knowledge that Brent was in love with her. But since that wasn't the case, she made the best of the situation and threw herself into the moment. Knowing that this would be her first and last marriage, no matter what the outcome, only made it that much more poignant.

Brent was stunningly handsome in his expensively cut, form-fitting Italian suit. The double-breasted jacket drew attention to his square shoulders and broad chest, and the slacks fitted his long, well-muscled legs like a glove. And as she stood next to him, reciting the vows that would bind them together, if only temporarily, she felt her heart swell with pride. He was not only physically breathtaking, he was the missing piece of her oft-broken heart. She couldn't imagine ever finding anyone who suited her so perfectly.

A surprising number of people attended the wedding: the entire, rabidly curious WCH crew had turned out in droves; Dr. Hanson and his wife; most of the birthing class, who were astonished to find that the Clarks had never been married; a staid but beaming Nurse Shocktaag; several people from Brent's apartment building; little Meg and a tearfully joyous Margaret were all in attendance.

Though she'd only managed to spend a few hours with Brent's mother the evening before the wedding, Elaine had instantly loved her. It was no wonder Brent was such a marvelous man. And, call it woman's intuition, Elaine believed that the feeling was mutual. The fact that Margaret was wild about Meg only served to clinch the bond between the two women. Brent practically had to drag Margaret back to his place, where they'd spent the night. Teasingly, he'd told Elaine that it was bad luck to see the bride before the wedding, and after a lingering kiss that she was sure was mostly for his mother's benefit, he'd promised he'd see her at the altar.

And he'd kept his promise. They were man and wife. Elaine could scarcely believe her good fortune. After a small reception in The Old Church's basement, the newlyweds had climbed into the waiting limousine with Meg and Margaret and gone home to Elaine's.

"Surely, you can't be serious," Margaret said, her brows furrowing in consternation. "Why ever not? Even a day or two in the country would be better than nothing," she said, referring to Brent's announcement that they hadn't planned a honeymoon.

Glancing self-consciously at Elaine, Brent struggled for the words that would satisfy Margaret's obvious mortification. They hadn't planned a honeymoon because they weren't really married. At least not that way. At least not yet. But he couldn't tell that to Margaret.

Thank heavens she was staying at his place for the next few days. It would be impossible to explain the fact that he would be sleeping on the couch on his wedding night. Someday, hopefully sooner than later, he would rectify this painfully inconvenient situation, but not before Elaine was ready.

"Mom, since this is our first Christmas together as a family, Elaine and I thought it would be nice to stay home, you know, with the tree and the gifts and start some traditions of our own with Meg." Shooting a beseeching look in Elaine's direction, he nodded imperceptibly, encouraging her to back him up on this matter.

"Yes," she murmured, blushing furiously at him. "We, uh, wanted to spend the night, uh, together, uh, here, at my... our house here in, uh, the—our bed." She plucked nervously at the petals of her corsage.

Meg squirmed in Margaret's arms as the woman looked back and forth between her son and new daughter-in-law.

"That's just plain silly. Allow me to play the part of interfering in-law for a moment here and say that I think you are making a big mistake. But, it's your life." She sighed dramatically. "If I can't convince you to get away for a day or two, at least go out to dinner. I can take care of the baby. Please. I want to."

Cuddling the baby in her arms, Margaret tilted her head and planted a grandmotherly kiss on Meg's chubby cheek. Striding to the couch in Elaine's living room where she'd deposited her purse after the wedding, Margaret withdrew her billfold and tossed a credit card at Brent.

"Here. Take your beautiful new wife out to dinner," she ordered. "I mean it now. I won't take no for an answer. We'll be just fine, won't we, lovey dover?"

Meg blew a row of bubbles across her rosebud lips and stared happily up at Brent's mother.

Brent turned to Elaine and shrugged. "You heard her."

Elaine nodded and smiled. "Thank you," she murmured as Brent helped her on with her coat. "We'll be back soon."

After quickly deciding where they would go for dinner and finding the phone number in the yellow pages, Brent gave his mother the lowdown on the ins and outs of baby care.

"Her diapers are in here, and I always put this white rash prevention stuff on her bottom before I change her, and she likes to play with Mr. Bunny, and if you hold her facing out, she's happier. Also—" he dragged a pensive hand through his hair "—she only cries really hard if she has a bubble in her tummy. So what I usually do is—"

"Brent. Get out of here. I took care of you for years and you managed to live to tell the tale. Don't give us another thought," Margaret advised, shooing them out the door.

They hadn't been gone ten minutes when the doorbell rang. Looking down at the baby, Brent's mother pursed her lips in dismay. "I can see your mommy and daddy are worrywarts," she cooed in baby talk, as she made her way to the foyer with Meg in her arms. Pulling open the front door, she opened her mouth to chastise them, but instead gasped in shock.

"*Amanda Johnson?*"

Chapter Twelve

Brent watched Elaine take a sip of her coffee in the dim light of the romantic little bistro they'd chosen for dinner, and couldn't believe his good fortune. This heavenly creature was his wife. His blood ran hot at the thought. And this was their wedding day. Correction, wedding night.

Brent shifted uncomfortably in his chair. The annoyingly efficient waiter who had hovered over their table through most of their meal was back, consulting Elaine about dessert. The dessert he had in mind wasn't available on the waiter's little tray of goodies. Oh, no. But it would be the perfect capper to the meal.... Good grief. If he didn't stop this train of thought soon, he'd spontaneously combust.

It was just that he'd never envisioned actually being lucky enough to find someone who fit his requirements so perfectly. Elaine was independent, career oriented, a great conversationalist, wonderful mother, sexy as all get-out, and considering they came from such different backgrounds, they thought a lot alike. They were remarkably simpatico. He couldn't even begin to imagine how lost he would be to her, once they'd made love. Although, he thought morosely, that probably wouldn't happen right away. If ever. Oh, damn, how could he stand it?

Shaking her head politely at the waiter, she lifted her darkly lashed eyes shyly up to Brent's and smiled softly. His pulse roared so loudly in his ears he was afraid she could hear it, too. They'd been somewhat bashful around each other ever since the wedding. The parameters of this new relationship would take some getting used to on both their parts, Brent knew. If he had his way, they'd spend this night in bed...exploring the parameters. By morning they'd both know where they stood. They would be husband and wife in every sense of the word.

"She said Zimbabwe this morning." Elaine beamed up at Brent.

He stared at her, trying to make the quantum leap from their marriage bed, back to the restaurant. What the devil was she talking about?

"Actually, it wasn't Zimbabwe, exactly. It was more like, Zzahhmmwe. Then she said, 'Ahhhhh, ahhhh, ahhhh, zzahhmmwe.' I think this bodes well for a career in news, don't you think?" Elaine twinkled mischievously at him.

Oh, she was talking about Meg. Brent gazed at her and smiled. Lordy, he loved the way she liked to chew on her luscious lower lip that way. It made the cutest dimples in the sides of her cheeks. Didn't she realize she was driving him nuts? Man, how he wished he could take his mother's advice about that honeymoon.

"I think she's brilliant and beautiful, like her mommy," Brent said, looking across the table at her through heavily hooded eyes.

Elaine colored girlishly. "Do you know that she is all we've talked about all evening?" Threading her fingers together, she rested her elbows on the table and supported her delicate chin with her hands, a smile playing at the corners of her mouth.

Only nodding because he wanted to remain agreeable, Brent suddenly realized that he didn't have much of a clue what they'd been talking about. Or what they'd eaten for that matter. All he could think about was taking his wife to bed.

"I was surprised at how many people turned out at the wedding today," she murmured, tilting her head at Brent and tossing her luxurious, shiny dark hair away from her delectable jaw. "The gang from the station really isn't so bad, once you get to know them."

"And once they get to know you. I think they've changed their tune about you since you had the baby." Brent wished he could push everything off the table onto the floor and take her right there. It certainly wouldn't be as comfortable as a hotel suite, but he wouldn't have to wait forever and a day to consummate this union, either.

For crying out loud. He was really beginning to lose it.

"If I'd known having a baby would have made me so popular at work, I might have done it years ago," she teased.

And, I'd have helped, Brent thought.

"You know, Brent, I really can't thank you enough for, well, you know . . . marrying me and Meg today." She studied her nails, embarrassed. "I know it was a real sacrifice for you, and I just don't know how I'm ever going to repay you."

Brent shifted self-consciously in his seat. She was making him out to be some kind of saint. She would be shocked if she knew how selfish his motivations had really been. Guilty at having deceived her this way, it seemed only fair to try to set the record straight. After all, she couldn't go around thinking he should be canonized. Especially considering the way he'd been mentally undressing her all through the meal.

"Elaine, it wasn't a sacrifice. I wanted to help, and I have lots of reasons." He sat back in his chair and toyed with the napkin in his lap. "I care a lot about Meg. I love her, actually." His gaze met hers. "And, I care a lot about you . . . in fact, I—"

"Would you care for some more coffee?" a voice behind him inquired.

"I, uh, oh, sure." Brent leaned out of the way to allow their waiter to refill his cup, and he mentally beat the tar out of the insensitive server. Couldn't the clod see that he was trying to tell the woman that he cared about her? Loved her even?

He sighed and smiled a thanks for the refill. It was probably better this way. The way he was going, he'd have spilled his guts and told Elaine how madly in love with her he was and spoiled any chance he had of winning her heart. He had to remember: slow and steady wins the race.

"How about you ma'am?"

"Sure." Elaine wanted to tear this idiot's head off. Couldn't the waiter see that Brent had been going to say something that would clue her in to how he felt about her?

She sighed and smiled a thanks for the refill. It was surely better this way. He probably had no intention of declaring his undying love for her. No, with her luck, he'd most likely been on the verge of asking for a raise or something equally impersonal. He could never really love her the way she'd come to love him. Why ruin a perfectly lovely honeymoon dinner with the truth?

She wanted him to kiss her.

As she stood on her front porch, fumbling through her purse for her house keys, Elaine was incredibly aware of the man who hovered at her elbow. Jolts of electricity seemed to fairly crackle between them. Couldn't he feel it, too? Maybe if she fiddled around long enough out here, before they went inside to relieve Margaret of her baby-sitting duties, Brent would haul her into his arms and kiss her into oblivion.

No, she decided—after rummaging for a ridiculously long period of time while her handsome husband stood patiently waiting—she'd been wrong. If anyone was going to haul her anywhere, it should be away. To the loony bin. She'd actually deluded herself into believing that this marriage was real.

Sighing in resignation, she withdrew her elusive keys and held them out to him. Somewhere along the way he'd lost his touch at reading her mind. Or, perhaps, she thought morosely, watching him unlock the door, he just didn't feel like kissing her.

Brent pushed the door open and echoed her sigh. He was beginning to think she'd never locate her blasted keys. It had taken every bit of his dwindling willpower not to grab her and kiss her into oblivion. But he knew that if he started, he wouldn't be able to stop. With his luck, Elaine would wallop him with her purse, and his mother would call 911. Resting a light hand at her back, he led them into the house.

Once inside they both stopped dead in their tracks and stared in shock.

"Amanda," Elaine blurted out and tightly gripped Brent's arm. For there, sitting cozily in front of the living room fireplace, bouncing a fussy Meg on her knee, was Amanda Johnson. And Margaret was nowhere to be seen. Exchanging worried glances, they quickly stepped into the room.

"You're back!" Amanda smiled up at them in greeting. "Good. I think she's hungry." Standing, she shrugged and held the whimpering Meg up to Elaine, as though it were the most natural thing on earth for her to be there, taking care of her granddaughter.

Elaine took the baby, who, back in familiar arms, stopped fussing and smiled.

"She sure knows her mommy," Amanda mused, shaking her head. "I tried every trick in the book, walking, singing, rocking..." She peered into the baby's face. "But you wanted mama, isn't that right my little punkin doodle?" Noticing Brent for the first time, Amanda shifted her gaze to him, and her eyes widened as though in recognition. She regarded him with interest for a moment. "You must be Brent."

"Where's my mother?" Brent asked, his jaw set grimly as he took a protective step toward his wife and child.

Amanda waved an airy hand. "Oh, we had a nice long, very enlightening chat, and then, since it was getting so late, she went back to your place. She says to tell you that she'll call you tomorrow about getting together for Christmas." Then, as though she didn't have a care in the world, she began straightening up the toys that lay strewn about the room.

Still rendered speechless, Elaine could only watch as Bobby's mother put the room back to rights and then retrieved and donned her white wool cape. Who was this woman? she wondered in amazement. She certainly looked like Amanda Johnson. She arched an incredulous eyebrow at Brent whose answering look spoke of his own misgivings.

"Your mother is...a good woman, Brent," Amanda stated calmly, as she turned toward him and flung her expensive wrap around her slender shoulders. "She tells me that, among other things, congratulations are in order." Her smile was sincere as she held her hand out to him.

Shooting another quizzical look at Elaine, Brent took the proffered hand. "Thank you."

Suddenly Amanda's expression turned melancholy. "I only wish I'd been half as understanding and sweet about my own son's marriage." Her eyes misted slightly. "But, it's too late for that now, isn't it?" Obviously not expecting an answer to her rhetorical question, she sniffed daintily and swiped at her eyes with her diamond-encrusted fingers.

"I'll be on my way and leave you two newlyweds alone now. But before I go, I just wanted to let you know that as a wedding gift of sorts, I'm going to call off the adoption proceedings."

Feeling suddenly light-headed, Elaine leaned against Brent's solid body for support. "That's wonderful," she breathed. Brent circled her waist with his arm and squeezed.

Amanda smiled softly at the family that stood before her, united by love. "I know Bobby would have wanted it this way. He was a beautiful man." She shook her head slightly, as if to clear it of her emotional turmoil. "It's apparent to me that little Meg here will be better off with two parents who love her, and each other, so much. I'm only sorry to have upset you both with all this in the first place, but I didn't know that my granddaughter was in such fine hands. I thought she might make up for losing him. And—" She stopped speaking for a moment, as tears of genuine regret trailed down her flawless cheek. "I miss him so much," she whispered.

"I know," Elaine murmured sympathetically.

Amanda swallowed and blinked rapidly up at the ceiling. "I've made a lot of mistakes in my life. I've been known to run over a person or two in my time to get what I want." She shifted her gaze back to Elaine. "But it's never really made me happy. Take it from me, Elaine. The love of a good man and a healthy baby are far more important than any other of life's status symbols."

Leaning forward and kissing Meg tenderly on her chubby cheek, Bobby's mother squeezed Elaine's arm, and then moved out of the room toward the foyer. She paused at the front door.

"If neither of you have any objections, I'd love to see her from time to time." Amanda inclined her head at Meg. "I'm in the book. Well—" Pulling open the front door, she stepped out into the brisk night air. "Good luck to you all."

And with that, she was gone.

The fresh pine scent of the Christmas tree filled Elaine with a sense of nostalgia as she sat curled up on the couch, covered with an afghan. It was such a beautiful tree. She couldn't remember the last time she'd bothered to decorate her home for the holidays. It had seemed so pointless without someone to share it.

Brent was in the kitchen, fixing them a glass of eggnog, and the sounds of his clumsily masculine activity brought a smile to her lips. She'd fed and put Meg to bed after Amanda had left. Staring at the tree, she watched the colored lights blink cheerfully from its limbs, and was taken back to another place and time.

A place and time where she had lain awake with Sara, urging her young cousin to listen closely—did she hear the reindeer landing on the roof? Sara had loved the game, wriggling with excitement and trying to convince Elaine that they should run downstairs and trap Santa Claus in the closet. That way they could rush to the roof and take a quick spin in his sleigh.

Sara had been such a delight. Both as a child and a woman. Elaine could only hope that Meg had inherited her cousin's free spirit. Someday, it would be her daughter listening for the reindeer. There was a sad poignancy to the thought that Sara's life had finally come full circle.

A log fell suddenly in the fireplace, drawing her eyes and sending a cascade of sparks swirling up the chimney. She'd never understood why Amanda hadn't liked Sara. Until tonight. She supposed the drive to climb to the top socially could do strange things to people. If anyone could understand the drive to climb to the top, she could, Elaine thought, self-deprecatingly. Thank heaven Brent and Meg had changed her priorities. It was clear to her now, that nothing was more important than family.

But what had prompted the sudden change in Amanda? Had the Ghost of Christmas Past visited her? Shivering, Elaine tucked the afghan more firmly around her legs and snuggled into the couch.

Maybe Brent would be able to shed some light on the subject, she thought, as he continued to forage noisily around her kitchen. His reporter's instincts were generally on the money. When had she grown so dependent on his thoughts and opinions? she wondered. She respected his input on everything from diaper rash to the state of the union.

It was then that it suddenly dawned on her that she had better get his input on the state of their union. Now that Amanda had called off her bid for custody, what reason did they have to stay married? None that she knew of, other than the fact that she was terminally in love with the messy guy in the kitchen, who labored so endearingly over his batch of eggnog.

That was why she decided, her heart heavy, that if he wanted out, she would let him go. Because she loved him. A marriage where only one of the people involved was in love was no marriage at all. When it came to Brent, she wanted all or nothing. But even that would most likely prove impossible. After all, she still had to work with the man. And then there was his relationship with Meg....

Oh, how would she ever be able to let go? *Please God,* she whispered, sending a silent prayer heavenward, *don't let him go.*

Back in the kitchen, Brent took a sip of the eggnog and frowned. Aside from the stuff Debbie called coffee at work, he'd never tasted anything so vile. It was no small wonder, considering he couldn't concentrate on anything except the possibility of losing the woman in the next room. The woman he'd come to love more than life itself.

But, after carefully weighing the situation, he knew that Elaine would probably see no reason to continue their marriage. As a quiet desperation settled in his gut, he struggled to come to terms with the fact that if she wanted out, he would have to let go. Elaine was not the type of woman to be forced into any situation. It was one of the things he loved about her. However, a marriage where only one person was in love, was no marriage at all. He would make the offer of freedom, only because he loved her. If she accepted, he'd know that it was the way it was supposed to be.

Pouring the disgusting eggnog down the drain, Brent wondered absently what it was that had changed Amanda's mind about the adoption. Was it something his mother had said? Whatever it was, in some respects he was grateful, and in others he was out of his mind with worry. Taking a deep breath he pushed himself away from the counter and snapped off the kitchen light. It was now or never, he decided and moved through the darkness toward the cheerfully crackling fire where his wife sat waiting for him.

"Hi," she whispered, and pulled her knees up under her chin to make room for him. "Where's the eggnog?"

"Busily eroding your kitchen plumbing," he quipped dryly as he sank into the couch and pulled her legs across his lap.

"That bad?"

"Mmm," he murmured, training his eyes on the flames.

They sat in silence for a moment, neither wanting to address the question that lay so heavily on their hearts. Finally Brent could stand the suspense no longer.

"Elaine," he began dully, still staring unseeingly at the fire.

"Hmm?" Something in his tone had her heart leaping fearfully into her throat.

"Now that Amanda has decided against adopting Meg, I was wondering...uh, just what you wanted to do about our marriage." *Please, God,* he prayed, *let her want it as much as I do.* Feeling duty bound by honor, he continued. "Uh, I could look into beginning divorce proceedings. Or, um, there is always annulment, I guess, considering that we never, uh...actually consummated the vows, and you know..." His voice trailed off miserably.

He sounded so miserable, Elaine wanted to curl up and die. The poor guy had really been through the ringer with her, she thought, studying his rugged profile in the firelight. As much as she wanted to throw a childish tantrum and rail against his words by kicking and screaming in agony, she knew it wouldn't be fair. Brent was the kind of guy who would stay with her out of a sense of duty. She couldn't allow it to go on any longer. It was time to let go.

Brokenhearted and not trusting herself to speak, she followed his eyes to the fire and nodded. Growing up, she had dreamed about and expected to be doing many things on her wedding night, with the man she loved, but discussing the dissolution of her marriage wasn't one of them.

"All right," she was finally able to whisper. "Do whatever you see fit."

His jaw grim in silhouette, he nodded quickly, not daring to look at her for fear he'd beg her to change her mind.

Elaine caught the movement out of the corner of her eye and bit her lip to keep from crying.

Chapter Thirteen

The holiday season had never seemed so bleak to Brent as he let himself into his apartment the next morning. He'd spent the night on Elaine's couch, unable to sleep and painfully aware that it would be one of his last nights under her roof. Preferring to avoid an awkward scene at breakfast that morning, he'd gotten up at the crack of dawn and headed home without seeing Elaine.

Soon he would need to pack his meager belongings and go back to his place to stay. It was hard enough contemplating not tucking Meg into bed each night, but when he thought about life without Elaine, well, it was decidedly more than he could bear. He'd made the fatal mistake of losing his heart to those two, and now he was going to have to pay the piper.

Shouldering his way through his front door, he kicked aside the pile of mail that had accumulated under his slot that morning and headed into the kitchen.

Margaret, who sat at his kitchen table browsing through

the morning paper, looked up from the cup of coffee she cradled in her hands in surprise.

"Hi, honey." Her smile was puzzled. "What on earth are you doing here? You're the last person I expected to see."

"Why's that?" Brent tried to effect a casualness he was far from feeling. After kissing his mother briefly on the cheek and pouring himself a cup of coffee, he joined her at the table.

"Need I remind you that last night was your wedding night? I thought for sure you would still be in bed recuperating from... your big night," she teased.

Brent shrugged and ran a weary hand across his jaw. He didn't find her attempt at humor particularly amusing this morning.

Sobering, Margaret reached out and squeezed her son's shoulder. "I get the feeling something's wrong."

Brent blew into his cup and took a sip of coffee. "Nah." He didn't feel like talking about it. He felt like punching something. But he couldn't. Margaret never had gone in for showy displays of temper.

"Would you like to talk about it?"

"No."

Margaret set her coffee cup down and, exhaling deeply, turned in her chair to face her son. "Brent." She swallowed and drew her cheek between her teeth, suddenly pensive. "I have a feeling I know what this is all about, and I think maybe I can help."

Brent's head snapped up sharply. "No, Mom. You can't, so just drop it, okay?" No amount of well-meaning, motherly advice could pull him out of this foul temper.

Sitting silently for a moment, Margaret appeared to make a decision. "Brent, I have something to tell you, and I want you to listen to me. I should have told you this a long time ago, but sometimes when things hurt too badly it's easier to just sweep them under the carpet and ignore them."

"Mom." Brent sighed. She never could take no for an answer. He knew she would tell him some cockamamie anecdote, designed to get him to spill his guts, and he wasn't in the mood. In an effort to spare them both, he decided there was no time like the present to come clean with her. She would eventually find out, anyway. "I'm not trying to sweep my troubles under the proverbial carpet. I'm just a little shell-shocked, that's all." He smiled wanly at her. "Elaine and I are going to get a divorce."

"What?" Margaret whispered in disbelief. *"Whatever for?"*

Beats the hell out of me, he wanted to say. "Because it never really was a marriage in the first place." At his mother's shocked expression, he hastily assured her. "Oh, it's legal, but the only reason we did it in the first place is because Amanda Johnson—you met her last night—"

Margaret nodded.

"She is Bobby's mother, and from what Elaine tells me, used to be a pretty rotten apple."

His mother's lips twitched.

"Anyway, she was threatening to file for custody of the baby. That scared the hell out of both of us. Luckily, her son Bobby had written a provision into the surrogate contract, stipulating that Elaine could keep the baby in the event that anything should happen to them—if she was married." He shrugged dejectedly. "So we got married. At the time it seemed like a good idea. And it must have worked, because last night, after we came home from dinner, she told us that she'd changed her mind about adopting Meg. So I guess something good did come of it after all."

Nodding, Margaret opened her mouth to speak, but Brent cut her off.

"Now there's no reason to continue the marriage." His eyes darted to his mother's. "Since Elaine doesn't love me, I decided to cut my losses and get out while my poor heart was still in one piece. Although," he mused morosely, "I'm beginning to have my doubts." His laugh was sharp. "Anyway, someday I'm sure she'll find someone to share her life with. Someone who will love her and Meg as much as I do."

Her expression full of sympathy, Margaret reached out and drew her son's large hand into hers. "She already has," she murmured.

Eyes dull, Brent stared at his mother. What was she talking about now?

"Honey," Margaret leaned forward, and something in her tone caught his attention. "I want you to listen to me for a moment. I have something to tell you, and in light of the circumstances, I think you should know. I was going to wait till after Christmas to tell you, but now seems as good a time as any."

What choice did he have? he wondered impatiently and nodded for her to continue.

"Last night, almost immediately after you two had left for dinner, there was a knock at the door. I thought you had a typical case of the parental jitters and had returned to give me some more instructions." She smiled. "But when I got to the door, I discovered Amanda."

Pausing, she took a deep breath, and then, as though she were afraid she might lose her nerve, her words tumbled out in a rush.

"I hadn't seen her in thirty-five years. Even so, I recognized her immediately."

Brent frowned. She wasn't making any sense. "Mom, what are you getting at?"

"Honey, she was the woman who took your father away from me."

"Amanda?" His brows knotted in consternation. Amanda Johnson was the evil socialite who had schemed and plotted her way into his father's life? To say he was shocked was certainly an understatement. The fact that Bobby and Amanda carried his father's surname certainly never would have tipped him off. Johnson was a very common moniker. It had never been his family name. Margaret had given him her maiden name when he was born.

"Mmm." Margaret nodded, and her eyes became glassy as she began unfolding the past to her son. "Amanda." Her voice took on a reflective quality. "I never expected to see her again. But in a way it was good for me. I think it gave me a sense of closure, after all these years of bitterness and jealousy. It also helped me realize that much of what happened was partly my fault."

Brent shook his head in disbelief. This was his mother speaking? He hardly recognized her. For once, she was talking about the past without turning beet red.

"Yes." She smiled at Brent's incredulous expression. "I gave your father to her without much of a fight. You see, I was convinced that he would be better off without me. Kind of like you and Elaine," she noted. "I regret that he never knew about you."

She sat in silence for a moment, remembering, while Brent attempted to digest this startling revelation.

"Why didn't you tell me this before?" he whispered, prodding her out of her reflective pose.

She lifted and dropped her shoulders. "I couldn't face the fact that I'd made a terrible mistake. It was easier to blame Amanda for everything. Anyway, you can imagine my surprise at finding her there on Elaine's porch last night, claiming to be Bobby Johnson's mother. Meg's grandmother. Well, I just couldn't let her stand out there on the porch without explaining herself. Not to mention the fact that I had the most childish urge to tear every platinum blond hair out of her head."

Brent grinned.

"So, I invited her in. She recognized me, too, after a while. We had quite the conversation. It was very healing." At Brent's skeptical look, she smiled. "Really. She told me that she and Rob—that's your dad—only had one child together. Bobby. I could tell, Brent, that she loved him and missed him very much. As much as I hate to admit it, I was actually beginning to feel sorry for her. So, I let her keep her hair and continue with her incredible story. She's really not so bad . . .

"I was saddened to learn that she lost Rob several years ago. He was your father, after all, and at the time I loved him very much."

Margaret's eyes misted over as she regarded her son. "You look so much like him. Amanda must have seen it, too. He was a very handsome man. Anyway—" she brightened "—Bobby would have been your half brother, and best of all, little Meg is your niece."

His niece? Brent's pulse roared in his ears. "That explains why everyone keeps saying she looks just like me."

"Well, come to think of it, she does," Margaret agreed. "I've got baby pictures of you that could certainly pass for Meg."

Brent felt as if he were dreaming. He'd always known that it was a small world, but *this?* Out of all the people in the world, Elaine Lewis, the woman he loved, had given birth to his niece. As disappointing as it was to discover that he'd had an entire family that he would never have the pleasure of meeting, he couldn't get over the fact that he was an uncle to the sweetest little girl in the world. Surely Elaine wouldn't prevent him from visiting his own niece.

"I could tell that even though Amanda was crazy about Meg, she wasn't really ready for the diapering routine again. We had a long talk, and I think I persuaded her that touring the world with an infant might put a crimp in her style." Margaret grinned. "She ended up admitting that the baby would be better off with you and Elaine, because you both love the baby—and each other—so much. And, I couldn't agree more."

Brent only wished his mother's words were true. "Mom, you're right. I do love Elaine. With all my heart. But she doesn't love me. To her, I'm just a friend seeing her through a difficult period in her life."

Margaret slapped the table with the palm of her hand so hard the coffee sloshed out of their cups.

"Are you crazy? That girl is head over heels in love with you, and if you can't see that, you are blind. Don't offer her a divorce, Brent. It's not what she wants. Please, learn from my mistakes. Don't give up the one you love because you are under the misguided impression that it's what they want." Her plea was impassioned. "I did that with your father. I could have fought for him. Instead, I rolled over and let Amanda have him. I guess, looking back, there is a silver lining to my cloud because now we have darling little Meg, and you have Elaine. But if I had it to do all over again, I would fight for my man. I only regret that he passed away before I could tell him that."

Completely stupefied by the incredible tale his mother had just told him, Brent could only sit and stare at her, numb with shock. Slowly his mind began to thaw, and he realized she was right.

He had to fight for Elaine.

Dammit, what did he have to lose? If he didn't take a chance and tell her how much he loved her, he'd lose her for sure. Besides, maybe she would consider staying married, once she realized that he, too, was related to the baby. Hell, considering the bizarre story his mother had just regaled him with, he could almost bring himself to believe anything.

Even the idea that—as his mother and Amanda seemed to believe—Elaine loved him.

Standing abruptly, Brent hauled his mother out of her chair and into his arms for a big bear hug. Setting her back down on her feet, he cupped her face in his hands and grinned.

"Thanks, Mom," he whispered. Before she could respond, he let go of her, spun on his heel and headed out to tell his wife how much he loved her.

He was gone.

Elaine stood in the middle of her living room and regarded the neatly stacked pile of Brent's belongings with apprehension. It appeared that he would be wasting no time moving out, now that they had agreed to dissolve their marriage. Her heart leaden, she turned toward the nursery, where Meg lay announcing to the world that she was hungry and, most likely, wet.

"Hi, little one," she cooed at the baby, who had looked at Elaine in surprise since her arrival and increased the pitch of her frantic wails. She wanted Daddy. Every morning, since the day she was born, Brent had made it his routine to get her out of bed and change her before he showered for work. Then he would stagger sleepily into Elaine's room and deposit Meg into Elaine's bed where she would nurse her back to sleep.

"I know, I know," she said, lifting the squalling baby into her arms and patting her gently on the back. "You want the guy with the mustache." She pressed her lips to the child's damp, wonderfully soft cheek. "I know how you feel."

Battling the tears that stung the backs of her eyelids, she settled into the rocker to feed Meg. "I want him, too," she whispered hoarsely.

Tomorrow was Christmas Eve. In the closet, hidden behind a pile of Meg's blankets, lay a pile of presents for Brent and the baby. Presents she'd wrapped with the tender care of a contented, deliriously happy woman in love. Over the past week, she had fantasized about their first Christmas together as a family, allowing herself this indulgence, even though she knew that it would never become a tradition. But she could dream. It had been years since she'd celebrated the day with family, and after years of lonely Christmases spent working at the station, she felt she deserved at least one holiday that she could reflect on in the forlorn years to come.

Now it seemed she could kiss even this slight consolation goodbye. At least she had Meg. But even though she loved this child with a mother's heart and soul, she would never get over losing Brent.

She'd never even had a chance to tell him how she felt. A bittersweet tear spilled over her lower lashes, down her cheek and onto Meg's. No, that wasn't exactly true, she amended to herself, as she stroked the dark fuzz at the nape of the baby's neck. She'd never had the courage to tell him how she felt.

What was wrong with her? She'd never have gotten anywhere in life, if she'd been this timid about everything. Top broadcast producers were generally never wilting lilies. Then why all the fear when it came to telling Brent how she felt about him? she wondered.

As she sat pondering this question, the answer began to make itself clear in her mind. Because she couldn't bear the thought of losing him. And secondly, because she was proud.

Well, she was losing him anyway, and her pride had already suffered a mortal blow, so what did she have to lose?

"Nothing," she stated so firmly that Meg started. "Sorry, honey," she said soothingly to the baby. "But Mommy just realized that she has to damn the torpedoes, so to speak and tell Daddy that she loves him."

"Zimbabwe," Meg babbled, then after a contented burp, went back to her meal.

"Elaine?" Brent let himself into her house with the key she had given him. Shrugging out of his jacket, he tossed it on the entry hall table and glanced into the empty living room. His heart sank as he noticed that she'd tidied up, removing all traces of his personal effects.

"In here," she called, and Brent followed the sound of her voice toward the nursery.

Rounding the corner to the baby's room, he found her there, slowly rocking their sleeping child. She smiled serenely up at him, and he felt his heart catch in his throat at the sight.

On the way over, he'd decided to skip the long, involved tale of Meg's family tree and cut to the chase. He'd wasted way too much time tiptoeing around the issue so far. She would either agree to remain his wife, or she wouldn't. It was a simple as that. And as complicated.

He stood in the doorway, opening and closing his fists, nervously wondering where he should start. It wasn't every day that he laid his heart on the line. All the words he'd so carefully rehearsed suddenly escaped him.

"Brent," she whispered, tensing slightly as she looked up at him. "I'm so glad you're back. I have something I need to say."

"Oh." She seemed so serious. Fear filled his gut. No. He couldn't let her speak before he declared his love. She might say something that would prevent him from accomplishing his mission. "That's great," he said, gripping either side of the doorjamb with his hands for support, "but first I have something to say to you...."

Interrupting, as though she hadn't heard him at all, she said, "And, I wish I had told you ages ago." She nervously touched the tip of her tongue to her lower lip.

That was fine with him. Right after he told her that he loved her. "That's great, honey. But first—"

"Although, I guess I was afraid to tell you that—"

Plowing a frustrated hand through his hair, Brent rested his forehead impatiently against the door. Couldn't the woman see that he was trying to tell her he loved her? Why did she have to choose this moment to drive him nuts with idle chitchat? He took a deep breath. He had to tell her that he loved her. Now. It was time. Whatever she had to say could wait. This couldn't.

"I love you," they both said in unison.

Exchanging shocked glances, they both asked, "What?"

"I love you," they answered together, then broke into matching radiant smiles, as they stared at each other in surprise.

"You do?" they whispered, then started to laugh. "Yes!" Their simultaneous declaration woke the sleeping Meg.

"Elaine!" Brent said, laughing as he crossed the room. "One at a time. Me first." Kneeling down beside the rocker, he cradled her cheeks in his hands and searched her face, the light of love and hope burning in his eyes. "Elaine Lewis, I love you. I've always loved you."

"You have?" she breathed, her eyes shining.

"Yes." He nodded solemnly. "And I want more than anything on this earth for us to stay married. Please say you will."

Her throat closed and Elaine was afraid she was going to cry. However, this time it wouldn't be from sorrow, but instead from spine-tingling, all-encompassing joy. She gazed up at the man who'd given so freely of himself and taught her the meaning of the word *love,* and then down at the tiny bundle in her arms. Nodding, she wondered how on earth she'd managed to get so lucky.

"Yes," she said when she was finally able to speak. "I can't think of anything I'd rather do than be wife and mother to you and Meg. I love you, too. Both of you." Lifting her tear-spiked lashes up to him, she promised, "With all my heart."

Groaning with relief, Brent pulled her close and covered her mouth with his.

And as he sealed their vows—to love, honor and cherish—Sara's voice echoed once more, deep in the secret shadows of Elaine's soul, granting her dearest Christmas wish and bringing her dreams to life.

Take care of them, Elaine . . . Came the whisper, soft and sweet. *They're yours now. Forever.*

Epilogue

"Good heavens, what is that horrible smell?" Amanda sighed in resignation as she glanced around at the happy mess that was the Clark household. Depositing several large bags of gifts on the floor, she removed her wrap and tossed it haphazardly over her booty. "When in Rome," she murmured and kicked off her pumps.

Kissing her on the cheek, Brent ushered her into the living room and placed the baby in her arms. "I sort of forgot about the turkey," he grinned. "I hope you like pizza."

"For Christmas?" She looked at the baby and tsked.

"That's what I say," Margaret said, emerging from the smoke-filled kitchen to join them in the living room. "Hello, Amanda." Smiling, she embraced Bobby's mother in welcome.

"Hi, Margaret. Where's Elaine?" Amanda asked, squinting through the haze.

"On the phone with Debbie and Ray. She's going to have them pick up a couple of pizzas on their way over." Pursing her lips, she scowled at her son.

Brent shrugged good-naturedly. "Hey, it was Elaine's idea to have me cook dinner. Being the liberated, working mother that she is, I've been trying to expand my culinary skills. I guess I have a thing or two to learn about preparing fowl...."

Amanda smiled. "I think you've mastered the art of foul."

A joyous squeal—coming from somewhere amidst the clouds that still belched from the oven—reached them only seconds before Meg did, her chubby legs pumping as she raced across the living room. "Grandma!" she shrieked in ecstasy as she hurled herself at Amanda's legs.

Amanda's face mirrored her granddaughter's delight. "Darling!" Handing little Bobby to Margaret, she bent down, scooped the excited Meg into her arms and planted loving kisses across her pink cheeks. "Was Santa good to you this year?"

"Yes!" she squealed. "I was a good girl."

"Most of the time, anyway," Elaine said with a smile, joining them and flapping a dish towel in an effort to clear the smog from the living room. "Hi, Amanda." After a quick hug, she tugged her excited daughter out of her grandmother's arms and set her on the floor. "Go wash up," she instructed her four-year-old bundle of energy. Turning to her guests she said, "I'm sorry about the turkey."

"Are you referring to your husband or our main course?" Margaret asked dryly.

"Both." Elaine giggled and Brent grabbed her around the waist and growled in her ear. "We've got pizza coming. And Dick and Mary are bringing a salad. If Liz and Danny bring dessert and Jason and Vicky bring something to drink we should have enough." She looked apologetically at the two grandmothers. "I hope that will be okay."

Amanda shrugged and nudged a pile of toys out of the middle of the floor with her foot. "It doesn't matter." She waved an airy hand. "To me, the important thing is family.

As long as we're all here together, I'm happy." She smiled contentedly at the Clarks.

"Here, here," Brent murmured as he nuzzled his wife's neck. "I couldn't have said it better myself."

* * * * *

COMING NEXT MONTH

#1132 SHEIK DADDY—Barbara McMahon
Super Fabulous Fathers

Years ago, Sheik "Ben" Shalik had loved Megan O'Sullivan with his whole heart. Now he was back, ready to sweep her off her feet. But could he forgive Megan for keeping their daughter a secret?

#1133 MAIL ORDER WIFE—Phyllis Halldorson
Valentine Brides

Mail order bride Coralie Dixon expected anything from her husband-to-be, except outright rejection! Handsome bachelor Jim Buckley *said* he wasn't interested, but his actions spoke differently....

#1134 CINDERELLA BRIDE—Christine Scott
Valentine Brides

Tall, dark and stirringly handsome, Ryan Kendrick was a perfect Prince Charming. But his "convenient" wedding proposal was hardly the fairy-tale marriage Cynthia Gilbert had been hoping for!

#1135 THE HUSBAND HUNT—Linda Lewis
Valentine Brides

Sarah Brannan was all set to say "I do." But then Jake Logan asked her to *live* with him—not marry him. So Sarah set out to turn the reluctant Jake into her willing groom.

#1136 MAKE-BELIEVE MOM—Elizabeth Sites
Valentine Brides

Prim and proper Laura Gardiner was shocked by rancher Nick Rafland's scandalous proposal. Nick needed a make-believe mom for his little nieces, not a real wife. But Laura wanted to be a true-blue bride....

#1137 GOING TO THE CHAPEL—Alice Sharpe
Valentine Brides

Elinor Bosley ran a wedding chapel, though she'd vowed never to walk down its aisle. Then she met sexy Tom Rex and his adorable four-year-old son. And Elinor started hearing wedding bells of her own!

**They're the hardest working, sexiest women in the
Lone Star State...they're**

Daughters
OF TEXAS

Annette Broadrick

The O'Brien sisters: Megan, Mollie and Maribeth. Meet them and
the men who want to capture their hearts in these titles from
Annette Broadrick:

MEGAN'S MARRIAGE
(February, Silhouette Desire #979)

The *MAN OF THE MONTH* is getting married to *very* reluctant bride
Megan O'Brien!

INSTANT MOMMY
(March, Silhouette Romance #1139)

A *BUNDLE OF JOY* brings Mollie O'Brien together with the man she's
always loved.

THE GROOM, I PRESUME?
(April, Silhouette Desire #992)

Maribeth O'Brien's been left at the altar—but this bride won't have to
wait long for wedding bells to ring!

Don't miss the DAUGHTERS OF TEXAS—three brides waiting to lasso
the hearts of their very own cowboys! Only from

 and ▼ *Silhouette* ROMANCE™

DOT

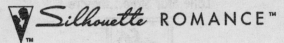

What do women really want to know?

Only the world's largest publisher of romance fiction could possibly attempt an answer.

HARLEQUIN ULTIMATE GUIDES™

How to Talk to a Naked Man,

Make the Most of Your Love Life, and Live Happily Ever After

The editors of Harlequin and Silhouette are definitely experts on love, men and relationships. And now they're ready to share that expertise with women everywhere.

Jam-packed with vital, indispensable, lighthearted tips to improve every area of your romantic life—even how to get one! So don't just sit around and wonder why, how or where—run to your nearest bookstore for your copy now!

Available this February, at your favorite retail outlet.

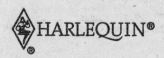

HARLEQUIN®

Cupid is on the loose...so bachelors beware, 'cause here come the

VALENTINE BRIDES

This February, Silhouette Romance invites you to spend the most romantic holiday of the year celebrating the joys of wedded bliss. Whether it's convincing that reluctant groom to say "I do" or advertising for a wife and mother—these special stories about love and marriage are the perfect Valentine's Day treat!

Don't miss:

#1133 MAIL ORDER WIFE by Phyllis Halldorson

#1134 CINDERELLA BRIDE by Christine Scott

#1135 THE HUSBAND HUNT by Linda Lewis

#1136 MAKE-BELIEVE MOM by Elizabeth Sites

#1137 GOING TO THE CHAPEL by Alice Sharpe

When Cupid strikes, marriage is sure to follow! Don't miss the weddings—this February, only from

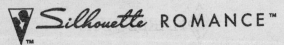

Silhouette ROMANCE™